# Ki knew there was only one way to win...

"This isn't the time for guns," Ki said in a quiet voice. "It's time to return to the old ways. We will fight silently. Kill silently."

There wasn't any more to say. There were no questions from the silent Utes.

"Now?" Jessica asked.

"There is no better time," Ki replied. "Jessie..."

"I'm going," she said.

"This isn't your type of battle. Hand to hand with men."

Jessie smiled. "It's my type of battle. It's against the cartel."

# WESLEY ELLIS

# LONE STAR

## AND THE
## WHITE RIVER CURSE

A JOVE BOOK

LONE STAR AND THE WHITE RIVER CURSE

A Jove Book/published by arrangement with
the author

PRINTING HISTORY
Jove edition/January 1986

ISBN: 0-515-08446-8

# LONE STAR

## AND THE
## WHITE RIVER CURSE

# Chapter 1

His name was Chi-Tha and he was a White River Ute. He had given up the ways of war to live in a green and peaceful Rocky Mountain valley where he now grew his corn, spoke to his spirits, and sometimes reminisced about the old days, days of valor glory.

Chi-Tha was seventy winters old now, still straight, lean, and with bright dark eyes. His hair was white and reached to his waist. He was no farmer, but his corn grew tall along the White River without much care. He could walk through acres of it, all of it to his head or higher.

A sound caused Chi-Tha to turn his head, to frown, and to start toward the rustling. Someone was in his corn again. If it was that little scoundrel, Pamda, he would pay this time.

An innate sense of caution caused Chi-Tha to unlimber the bow he had worn slung across his shoulder, to notch an arrow as he walked through the tall corn, smelling the ripe-

1

ness of it, hearing the humming of the bees.

"Pamda!" he called out, "Go home to your mother. Get out of my corn," but there was no answer, only an increased rustling. "Get out of my corn," the old Ute yelled again. Now he was angry, his warrior's blood stirring. He strode on determined to punish the interloper.

*It* burst from out of the corn and the sunlight shone on it. It rode a dark horse that gleamed like the White River. It had no face, the man-shaped thing, but it too shone. A long lance was in its hand.

The horse reared up. Chi-Tha leaped back. He knew suddenly what he was seeing. The old ones. One of the Spanish men, one of those who had come to conquer the Utes in their mountain stronghold and been driven away, one of those who had cursed the tribe, the blood of the Utes.

"Go away, ghost!"

But the thing would not turn back. The horse came on, clanking, shimmering, and the silent rider lowered the long lance he carried.

Chi-Tha was swift. He brought his bow up to waist level and fired. But the arrow only bounced off the ghost.

Again he fired, still backing away toward the river, but again the shaft of the arrow broke as it struck the faceless thing which had come to Chi-Tha's field. The old man turned and he ran, he ran knowing that he could not win against this spirit. He ran and behind him the ghost horse trampled the corn. He would die; Chi-Tha knew he would die. He reached the river, he plunged into it, and the current, swift now as the mountain snows melted, swept him away.

He had only a moment to look back to see the shining ghost before the White River carried him around the bend and away from his field.

· · ·

"What was that?" Beth Hicks asked.

Her husband yawned. He was tired. Hicks had worked his ranch on the White River for eleven years, and he worked six days a week from the time the sun came up until it went down. And more often than not times in between. He put his arm around his bulky wife and scooted nearer to her, but she shook him off.

"Grant Hicks, there's someone out there."

"Indians, I suppose," he muttered. Once there had been Indian trouble, long ago, before Hicks had brought his wife and daughter out to Colorado. Even then it hadn't been much, however; the Utes knew Hicks had come to work, to mind his own business. They knew he had come to stay, so after a few threatening forays they had left him alone.

"I don't know. Maybe the cougar come back," Beth Hicks said. She was no delicate flower, but a hefty, hard-working woman. She gave Hicks a shove that nearly sent him from the bed, but the rancher refused to rise.

"I'll see myself, Grant Hicks," the rancher's wife said. She rolled out and put on a nightdress. No matter what Hicks thought, *she* had heard something out there.

"What is it, Beth?"

As Beth Hicks stepped out of the bedroom their daughter, an eighteen-year-old girl with nice, if squat, proportions and fine, long dark hair, came to meet her.

"Did you hear something, too, Charlotte?"

"I," the girl hesitated, "think so."

"Yes, well, so did I. Pap's either tired or being lazy. Let's look. Grab the rifle."

Charlotte Hicks nodded resolutely, crossed the cold room, and took the Henry repeater from its wooden pegs above the stone fireplace.

"Now, you get to bed," the older woman said.

"No." The girl was determined as her mother. "You go

3

first and I'll come along."

"Right." Beth Hicks levered a .44-40 cartridge into the rifle and started toward the door. Outside it was clear, starry, and cool as it always was at this elevation.

Beth Hicks said with a shrug, "I don't see anything. Guess the old man was right."

"Th–there," Charlotte Hicks said, and her finger jabbed at the darkness. Then Beth saw it, too, and she did something she tried not to do in front of her daughter, she cursed slowly, profusely.

"Son-of-a-bitch," the frontier woman added as final punctuation.

Well, it was enough to make a saint cuss. There was a dark figure among the horse herd, and it was no Indian. What it was . . . was a knight in armor.

A knight in armor, the starlight gleaming dully on his accoutrements. Now, his eye drawn by the appearance of the two women, he wheeled his huge armor-clad horse and rode through the horse herd which milled and snorted and then broke into a stampede.

The dark herd broke through the corral bars and raced toward the open valley beyond. The knight, dark and eerie, pushed them ahead of him. He lifted a lance and waved it menacingly at Beth Hicks.

And she shot him.

She lifted that Henry and fired. The bullet rang off the metal the rider wore, but he was stunned by it. That was obvious by the way he reeled in the saddle and then turned his horse to go clanking off into the night, a second shot from the Henry repeater following him.

For a long while then Mrs. Hicks and her daughter stood watch on the porch, but the knight didn't return. "I think that bullet tagged him a little harder than we thought," Beth Hicks said with a little nod of satisfaction. "All right, now, it's getting cold. In to bed."

She slapped her daughter affectionately on the rump and sent her into the house. Beth started to follow, but just for a moment she paused and looked toward the darkness before shaking her head in wonder.

"No," she told herself, "wasn't a dream at all."

Returning to bed, she nudged her husband and crawled in. "What wazzit?" Grant Hicks asked sleepily.

"What it was was a knight in armor, Grant Hicks," Beth said, sitting up, pushing his shoulder roughly.

"Come for Charlotte?" her husband asked from under the quilt.

"What? Oh. No, not a knight in shining armor come for our daughter! It was . . . hell, you'll find out in the morning when you wonder where your horses are."

In the morning Grant Hicks wondered where his horses were. He went in to his wife who was cleaning up after breakfast and demanded that she tell him. She did with some dark pleasure.

"The well's been poisoned," Grant told her. "Laugh that off." He reached for his coat and hat—and the Henry repeater.

"Where are you going now?"

"Going to town, Beth. I'm going to report this to Carl Dant."

"The marshal will laugh himself silly. You'll make a fool of yourself."

"I don't give a damn about that. I'd rather be a fool than be driven off this land. What is going on around here, anyway? That's what I'd like to know."

Carl Dant wondered the same thing. The marshal of Sharpsville had the job because the citizens hadn't been able to find anyone else who would take the job and stay sober. Dant was lazy, useless, red-headed, lean, and dirty. He

5

suited the town fairly well.

He turned his head, spat tobacco juice on the office floor, and looked again at the lanky, sober rancher across his scarred desk.

"What is going on around here, anyway?" the marshal intoned. He stretched his arms overhead and yawned.

"That's what I come to tell you. My wife says a man in a suit of armor raided my place last night. He let down the corral rails and—"

Marshal Dant held up his hand. "I know that, Grant, you told me twice. Thing you don't realize is I'm a town marshal. I can't come down to your ranch for something like this."

"What the hell are you paid for, anyway?" Grant Hicks asked hotly.

"You know what I'm paid for." The marshal spat again, seeming to take delight in his aim. "For upholding the peace in Sharpsville. Don't have a thing to do with you White River ranchers. The three of you got to fend for yourselves. I've already talked to Ralph Wertz—"

"Wertz!"

"Yes, and if you fellows didn't feud about his son and your daughter maybe you could have caught this fool in this steel suit."

"You can't mean Wertz saw him, too."

The marshal nodded. "That's what I do mean." The law-man creaked forward in his chair. "You act like you didn't believe your wife."

"You know women," Grant Hicks said meekly. "Middle of the night . . ."

"I don't know women," the marshal said obliquely. "All I know is this ain't my duty. You and Wertz and the Utes will just have to take care of it yourselves."

6

"The Utes?" Grant Hicks shook his head. "He's bothered them, too?"

"So Chi-Tha says. Know him, do you? Says he had to swim five miles in cold water because a ghost chased him from his cornfield."

"A ghost?"

"Don't you know them White River Utes once killed a bunch of Spanish men hundreds of years back. The last Spaniard that was killed put a blood curse on them. Chi-Tha figured that this was the Spanish ghost come back."

"Ignorant savage."

"As ignorant as thinking a knight on horseback is wandering around. Say, you know something." The marshal stood. "I got some kind of a letter about three months ago . . ." He went to his files, which were wads of papers and wanted posters stuffed in a whiskey crate, and started digging through.

Hicks stood watching him, frowning in confusion.

The marshal said, "Some woman, name of Starbuck or something, in Texas said she wanted to know if there was any strange activity in this valley. Strange! If this ain't strange, I don't know what—here 'tis!"

The marshal rose with a creak of knee joints and a sigh. "There." He showed Hicks the letter. It was faded and torn.

"What am I supposed to do with this?" Hicks asked as the marshal pressed the letter on him.

"Write! There's a letter. The lady says she wants to know if anything strange happens along the White River."

"But why?" Hicks asked, peering at the letter. "Who the hell is Jessica Starbuck and what does she want to know about anything this far away for?"

• • •

Jessica was behind her father's desk at the Starbuck Ranch when the letter, scrawled in crooked lines, arrived from Colorado. She opened the letter with her father's old scrimshaw letter opener. She had a sudden vivid memory of that instrument in his powerful, square hand. Long ago. Before they had taken him and killed him.

She slowly read the letter and then read it again, puzzled.

After she put the letter down on the old oak desk, she just sat, meditating. Even in meditation she was lovely, but when she was in motion, riding across the vast ranch, laughing, then the woman became an astonishing thing.

She had long honey-blond hair and sparkling sea-green eyes, a quizzical, kissable mouth, and body, lush and ripe, that every woman envied silently and men wanted. But she belonged to no man, except possibly to the one called Longarm, the one who was far from Texas now, following his own bloody trail.

"Jessica?"

She looked up to see a tall man in the doorway. Ki was half-Japanese, half-American. He was a very special kind of warrior, trained in a dozen Oriental fighting skills. He was a very special kind of friend.

"Come in, Ki."

"Something important has arrived?" the tall man asked, crossing the room.

"Have a look," Jessica shrugged. She stood and roamed the room while Ki scanned the letter. When he was through, he looked up.

"The cartel."

"Doesn't it have to be?" the woman asked. "Remember the dispatch from Karl Fordham."

"That was quite a while back, Jessie."

"Yes, but that letter Karl came up with was quite specific. The cartel wants the White River Basin. You'll remember

8

there were six targets listed in that letter to their agent. The White River Basin was number one. I think they've laid off it because they suspected the letter was intercepted. Now they've made up their minds to go in."

Ki nodded. He placed the letter down on Alex Starbuck's desk top. Alex Starbuck had been a merchant king and was murdered by members of an international criminal ring called the cartel. He had left his wealth and his resources to Jessica, his daughter.

Alex Starbuck left Jessie a sense of duty and honor and a lasting hatred of the cartel that wanted nothing less than to colonize America economically and make this new, still forming, sprawling and prospectively wealthy nation its own.

"Why the knight in armor?" Ki wondered, glancing again at the letter. "It is a bizarre method."

"I don't know, but however the cartel men are dressed, they are succeeding in frightening the residents."

"Indian and white mixed together?"

"Apparently there are just three ranchers, Ki, and they've always gotten along well. But if this continues I can imagine who the Utes will blame."

"The ranchers," Ki agreed. "Wanting to push them from their land."

"It's an unhealthy situation anyway." She paused. "And it's one the cartel would revel in. I think we have to go out there."

"If it's what you wish," Ki said and he rose. What Jessica wanted she got. Her instincts had been unerring in the past, and if she believed it was the cartel at work, then it very likely was.

Still, the man in armor bothered Ki.

Ki, who was a warrior, had seen men fight in armor before. Samurai in his native land with their swords and bright armor still fought ritual battles. But with the coming

9

of gunpowder, armor had become an anachronism, ponderous, slow, compared to Ki's own way of warfare, *te*, the way of the empty hand, swift and deadly.

In America there never had been armored warriors except briefly, centuries ago, in the southwest, the *conquistadores*. Ki didn't like the implications. There were alternatives— hallucination?—illusion?

Madness.

Who but a madman would wear armor in the western mountains of America?

"Ki?" Jessica's voice broke in on his thoughts. "We can have a buckboard take us to the railhead within the hour. There's a train leaving this afternoon. Are you ready?"

"I'm ready," Ki said and still he frowned. There was a doubt lingering in the back of his mind. For Ki, who had mastered many ways of fighting and the use of many weapons, knew there were no good weapons to use against madness.

Two hours later they were on a train rolling west. Texas, brown and golden and occasionally green, flat and limitless, rolled past.

Ki briefly closed his eyes as the golden light of the falling sun winked through the train window into his eyes. He closed his eyes and saw the soft spring of Japan, the time before. He seemed to see his mother's face, to hear her. She who had been highborn but scorned because she had married a barbarian, an employee of Alex Starbuck. She had suffered with dignity in a way Ki had never learned entirely.

He had been an outcast from birth, mocked for his white blood, and perhaps that was what had driven him to join a monastery, to devote himself to the grueling regimen of the martial arts.

He had come to America hoping to find a civilization

10

which would treat him as a whole man, not as a half man. He had heard the name Starbuck, so he had gone to this great man and he had been hired. Starbuck had called him his foreman, but Ki was nothing more nor less than Jessie's bodyguard and tutor—for she had learned a little of the empty hand way of fighting. Now he hoped he was more than a bodyguard, more than a tutor. He hoped they were friends.

But he was her warrior, her protector. He would lay down his life for her and had put himself on the line for her more than once. He would do it again, for Ki was a man of honor and he had promised Alex Starbuck.

He would not forget such a vow.

Let the enemy be a cartel thug, a gunman, a savage— or a knight in armor, and he would find himself dealing with Ki.

Ki opened his eyes briefly and he saw Jessie there, silhouetted against the bright window, her head held high, her mouth determined and yet vulnerable, her throat sleek and smooth, her breasts full and proud.

She must be protected. She must survive, and she would so long as Ki lived.

He closed his eyes and the train rumbled on across the vastness of the Lone Star State.

★

# Chapter 2

The Rockies were a vast, towering tangle of deep, blue mountains capped by snow and lost in the haze of distances above the tiny, forlorn town of Sharpsville.

Sharpsville had been born to die. A trading post, briefly an army garrison, and during an empty boom a mining town, there wasn't much left but the general store and two saloons, doing business as such places always seemed to do.

The stagecoach rocked to a halt in front of the hotel. The Colorado House was converted from an assayer's office. Compartmentalized for a Chinese madame and her troop, it had ceased long ago to be a series of squeaking, stinking cribs and existed now only for the occasional befuddled, lost traveler who had wandered to Sharpsville.

The wind was blowing hard when Jessica Starbuck stepped on to the muddy street of Sharpsville, Colorado and stood looking at the bleak town.

Ki followed her and waited while the driver threw down their bags.

Jessie, in a green riding jacket and skirt, white silk blouse and flat crowned hat, was drawing the eyes of every man on Sharpsville's one and only pretense of a street. She enjoyed it, appreciated it in a peripheral way, but it was such a part of her life to be looked at by men that she hardly noticed it.

"Can you tell me where we can find the marshal's office?" Ki asked the stage driver.

"You can find it right there," he pointed, "next to the livery. Whether he's in there or not I can't say."

"If he isn't?"

"Try the Golden Horn. They've got the cheapest whiskey in the territory."

The driver started his stage forward, guiding it toward the livery himself. It was time to switch teams and grab a bite to eat before turning around and heading back down the winding mountain road.

"Let's have a look," Jessie said. Ki picked up their luggage and they crossed the rutted street to the marshal's dilapidated office.

Inside, it smelled of tobacco, raw whiskey, and unwashed man. The marshal was asleep behind his desk, arms crossed, boots propped up. Ki dropped their baggage and as it hit the floor one red eye opened.

"Yeah?"

"Marshal Dant?" Ki asked.

"That's right, what is it?" Then his reddened eye lit on Jessie and his boots hit the floor as he came to his feet, palms brushing futilely at his stained, dusty vest. "Well, howdy, miss. Thought it was just the China boy here."

"He's Japanese and American," Jessica said, removing

14

her hat to shake her hair free. "No matter what he is, it's hardly a reason for rudeness."

The marshal looked sly and abashed at once. "No, miss," he said. A hand gestured, "Take a seat and tell me what I can do for you."

Jessie ignored the invitation to sit. "What you can do is tell me where I can find a man called Grant Hicks and tell me what you know about a man in medieval armor who's been raiding the local ranchers and Indians."

The marshal nodded slowly. Paring a wad of tobacco from a block of plug cut, he tucked it in his jaw and said, "So you're that one. So you're Starbuck's kid."

"You knew him, did you? Knew my father?"

"No." The marshal wagged his head and spat. "Heard the name, that's all. I ain't had lunch with the President, but I know his name, too." The marshal seemed to find that cleverly amusing and he chuckled a little. Jessie didn't like the man and wanted to get to the point.

"What can you tell me about this, any of it, Marshal Dant?"

The man shrugged again. "Nothin' that warn't in Hicks's letter. He told it all."

Ki stepped forward, "Surely you have investigated—"

"I don't investigate out of the town limits, mister." He spat once again, his eyes showing delight as he apparently hit a target. "I investigate Sharpsville from one end to the other. You want to investigate, you investigate." The marshal had gotten stuck on that word.

"Can you tell us where Hicks's ranch is?" Jessica Starbuck asked.

"I can—I *will*," the marshal answered, amusing himself again. "Step outside, look at the mountains. Head south, sticking between the mountains and the White River. Ten

15

miles down you'll find Hicks."

There wasn't much to do but thank the man and get out of the rank office.

"I'll see about hiring horses," Ki said. "Do you want a buckboard as well?"

Jessie glanced at the luggage. "I think so."

Ki started off, leaving Jessica to stand and look at the tall mountains, the intimidating, thrusting peaks. She put her hat back on and sat on her trunk, the trunk which contained her jeans and rough-country clothes, her double-action Colt .38 revolver with the polished peachwood grips, and most importantly the black book.

The black book which listed the names, and sometimes the locations and occupations of members of the cartel, the killing, bloody cartel. Folded inside the book was the letter that had been captured by Karl Fordham, a private operative working in the east. The letter which pinpointed the White River Basin as a cartel target.

Even from here it was easy to see why they might want it. Beyond the dingy, rotting town, the valley spread out, fertile and wide and green, running nearly half the length of the wandering river. It was prime cattle country. Jessie who had been raised on the Lone Star Ranch knew what such water and grass would be worth.

She knew also what the Civil War had done to the price of beef, as did everyone in the east who had to buy it. Beef was high and the railroads were coming. There was no estimate on the value the White River Basin could one day have—to the Utes and handful of old settlers *or* to the cartel.

Ki hadn't returned yet, which was a little surprising, but Jessica Starbuck knew him too well to be worried. He could handle himself as few men could. She yawned, wrapped her locked fingers around one knee, and sat watching early dusk come in, creeping over the basin rim to flood the valley

16

with deep purples and deeper blues.

Ki still hadn't returned.

Inside the stable it was dark and still. Ki called out again for the hostler, but there was no one there. Outside the weary stagecoach horses waited to be rubbed down and grained, but no one was doing that.

"Hello!" Ki called again.

He spotted the buckboard against the back doors and decided to save time by finding the harness he would need. Probably the stablehand had gone to eat and would be back shortly.

Walking along the plank wall to his right, Ki looked at the various tack. Occasionally a horse whickered. A big white gelding methodically kicked the back wall of his stall with his hind hoof.

The small side door opened and two men were briefly framed there.

"Hello," Ki said, turning that way, "I've been waiting for you."

But an instinct, a warrior's knowledge, flashed a warning signal inside Ki's skull. These were not hostlers, not working men. They had come with other thoughts in mind. They wanted to hurt, perhaps to kill. Ki stopped, frowning, feeling his muscles bunch.

Deliberately he relaxed, breathing in a slow, measured way, slowly clenching and unclenching his fingers.

"I have been waiting for the stableman. Do you know where I can find him?"

"In hell," one of the men, a deep voiced, ponderous man suggested.

"That's too far to go," Ki said, trying to keep it light, to pretend that he did not sense menace, while his eyes searched the dark, musty interior of the stable, while he

17

peered through the murkiness at the two huge men approaching.

"Maybe so, maybe no," the bigger one said. "It's a quick trip, my friend."

"Perhaps," Ki said in a way that was quiet but also meaningful. But these men were too intent on their work, too sure of themselves to hear the menace. They were not the kind to recognize in Ki a warrior more skilled than themselves. They had guns; they would kill.

"Perhaps," Ki said, "a man would not care to make that journey alone."

"What's that mean?"

"Perhaps he would like to have the company of his murderer—think twice."

The smaller man laughed out loud. He had a dark rain slicker, although the day had been dry, and a dark hat. His raincoat was drawn back to show twin pistols.

"He's threatenin' us, Barge. He's goin' to take us with him. Chinaman ain't even got a gun."

"No," Ki said, "I have no gun."

What he did have was *shuriken*, star-shaped throwing knives that these men had never seen, that they would not fear if they did see them. Inside of Ki's sleeve was a spring-loaded mechanism that needed only a small movement on his forearm muscles to fill his palm with cold, deadly steel.

Now Ki activated the mechanism, the small sound the mechanism made going unnoticed by the assassins, as they walked unnoticing past crickets and scuttling lizards, all of the softer sounds a man with trained senses hears, sees, *feels*.

It was the smaller man who tried it. Ki saw him slap at his right hand holster, saw the gun come up. A flick of Ki's wrist sent the *shuriken* whistling toward the gunman.

It caught him under the wrist, ripping tendons, and with

18

a shriek the thug fell back, his Colt dropping to the floor of the stable. He was holding his wrist, almost stemming the heavy flow of blood.

The one named Barge had hesitated, seeing his partner struck by a menace he couldn't even see. He paused before he drew and Ki merely stepped in, lifting his leg, striking out with a sharp kick, which caught Barge under the throat and snapped his head back.

Barge, his tongue protruding, his eyes goggling, went down hard. The other one was running toward the door and Ki let him go.

"Here, what's going on!"

Ki turned toward the front door where a man with a limp and a receding chin was making his way forward.

"What are you doing here?"

Ki answered, "Merely trying to hire a buckboard and two horses."

"Yeah?" The stableman's eyes narrowed and focused on Barge who lay lumped against the dark stable floor. "And what's he doing there?"

"I have no idea." Ki shrugged. "Probably drunk."

"Drunk? Ain't dead, is he?"

"No," Ki answered. Although the man could easily have been killed by that kick designed to crush the trachea, he had only collapsed.

The stableman hunkered down, gave a little muttered oath, and said, "Barge Haycox."

"A well-known tippler," Ki suggested.

The stableman rose, wiping his hands. He studied Ki cunningly. "Yeah. And a well-known gunman. What was it you wanted?"

"A buckboard and a team."

The man with the limp nodded and got to work. Ki paid him in gold, promised to send the buckboard back when possible, and drove out into the dusk of Colorado.

Jessica looked a little impatient.

"Sorry." Ki leaped down, helped the blonde up, and threw their luggage in the back of the buckboard. "The stableman was out."

"And?" Jessica asked and Ki smiled.

"Am I that transparent? *And* I was attacked by two men."

"How could they know already?"

"The cartel? If it was them, I don't know. Except," he said, climbing back into the wagon box, "we are a remarkable pair. Perhaps they only wanted to rob me."

"Perhaps," Jessie said, but neither of them believed it.

They knew. The cartel knew that they had arrived, and although it meant that the danger of death was nearer, it was also perversely satisfying to Jessica to realize that they had guessed right. This was the battlefield, this beautiful long valley where scattered oaks grew in staggered ranks along the wandering, broad river. There was grass as far as Jessica could see and as they drove farther south they began to see beef cattle with a brand they deciphered as Tilting H.

"Hicks," Jessie said aloud. "This must be his place already."

That guess was confirmed by the smoke they saw rising from a small stone house a mile on and by the light shining in the windows of the house.

They rode up the narrow trail past curious horses, blank faced cows, and a pair of pale donkeys. The front door opened as they rolled into the yard, and a man with a rifle in his hands stepped out, the room bright with lamplight behind him.

Ki winced. Why did men do that? Didn't he realize that he made a target of himself by doing that? Well, Hicks was no warrior. Ki hoped he also was not a fool, for they needed help and they hadn't gotten any from the local law.

"Who are you?" the man on the porch called out.

"Grant Hicks?" Jessie asked.

"That's right."

"We've come to talk about knights in armor."

"You have, have you?" He paused. "Well, come on in."

Hicks wasn't a fool. He hadn't much education, but talking to him Ki and Jessie had the idea he was clever enough. So were his wife and rather plump young daughter. All of them were certain of what they had seen.

"The second time he came he just rode past the house at a gallop, clanking and rattling," Hicks said describing the knight.

Ki asked, "He returned a second time?"

"Him or another like him. There seems to be more'n one because Ralph Wertz, who's got the place south of here, was hit the same night I was. He wasn't so lucky. He lost a lot of hay and his barn."

"Why is someone doing this?" Jessie asked.

"They want the land. It's that simple," Hicks believed.

That was Jessie's own evaluation; she had wanted to hear it from Hicks's lips, however.

"The more important question is why someone would dress up in armor to try this," Ki thought. He looked to the fire, which burned brightly in the fireplace. "Why and *how?* People don't normally own armor. Even to dress in such a costume requires much help."

"And where did he come from?" Jessie put in. "He can't be riding out from town every night, can he?"

"No. It's got to be from over the ridge," Grant Hicks said.

"Camden," his wife agreed.

"What's that?" Ki wanted to know. He shifted in his chair, smiled at Charlotte Hicks who turned away, blushing, and returned his attention to Grant Hicks.

21

"Little town over the hills. Nothing there. A man came through a month or two back though and said something was going on. It's not far over the hills, a lot closer than from here to Sharpsville."

"And the trail's not traveled," his wife put in.

Jessica leaned forward, her hands wrapping around the coffee cup they had given her. Her green eyes were bright with firelight. "Have you tried following his man, tracking him to see if your theory is correct?"

"Nope," Hicks said with finality. "Didn't try to follow him, don't want to. I want to be left alone to work and mind my own business. If he comes back, I'll shoot at him again; as for running around the hills looking for him, no thank you."

"Then I guess," said Jessica Starbuck, "it's something we'll have to do for ourselves."

She glanced at Ki, who nodded and smiled faintly. Yes, it was something they would have to do, but there was an air of unreality about it which caused Jessie to have some of the misgivings that Hicks apparently felt. Chasing a dark knight across the dark hills was just a little fantastic for the mind to accept totally, and that night as they slept in the Hickses' house Jessica Starbuck suffered through a long series of dreams where skull-faced knights fought to the death in armored combat.

# Chapter 3

Morning was bright, cool. They ate breakfast with the Hicks family and then were given two saddle horses. "Momma and Charlotte are going into town tomorrow," Grant Hicks told Jessica and Ki. "They'll take back the stable team and buckboard."

"We appreciate it," Jessie said. She was tugging on a pair of soft riding gloves. She now wore a faded denim jacket and denim jeans, which molded themselves deliciously to her bottom. "If we have to get over the hills, the buckboard won't be much use."

"If you folks want," Hicks said cautiously, "I can take the day off and come along, show you things."

His manner indicated that was the last thing in the world he wanted to do so Jessie politely declined. "I think what you sketched out last night will be enough to get us around. South of you is the Wertz place, then the J-Bar which belongs to Al Jankowitz. From there it's Ute land the length of the valley."

"That's it," Hicks said, watching as Jessie swung aboard. He paused. "You be careful, young lady. I don't know what these people want, but I don't think they're doing it for amusement. I got the feeling that they can play rougher than they have been, quite a bit rougher."

"That," Jessica Starbuck said, "is the same feeling I have, Mr. Hicks."

She waved to the two women on the porch and with Ki rode out of the small, prosperous ranch, down the long valley, which broadened still more until it was five miles wide. Above them to the west was a low line of hills, still in shadow, and farther up were the Rocky Mountains, the snow-tipped peaks catching the early sunlight and reflecting it brilliantly. Several doves winged across the valley and twice they spotted mule deer.

"Yes," Ki said meditatively, "it would be worth it."

"There are only the three ranchers," Jessie pointed out. She had some other meaning.

Ki prodded her. "Yes?"

"And the Utes. Who would the Utes blame?" she asked.

"The ranchers, probably. Who else would want to drive them off this land."

"And if the Utes did try to retaliate, then there could be trouble, enough trouble to have them pushed off their land and put on a reservation."

"Maybe." Ki walked his horse across a bright silver rill, which wound its way across the grassland. "It is plausible, but we don't know enough to say that this is what is intended."

"Something dirty," Jessica Starbuck said, "is damn sure intended."

"Perhaps the men following us also intend something

dirty," Ki said, and Jessica turned in the saddle.

"We're being followed?"

"Someone rides the same way," Ki answered. "Someone who rides cautiously."

But there was no way the men could catch up or cut them off, so they chose to ignore the possibility that they were being stalked. For the time being.


Ralph Wertz was a strapping man with a strapping red-faced son. Both of them were pounding nails into the green lumber of their new barn when Jessica and Ki rode up. Wertz and his son swung down.

They had rifles with them and Wertz had picked his up. His son was too busy gazing goggle-eyed at the lush figure of the honey-blonde.

"Wertz?" Jessie called.

"Yeah, who wants to know?"

"I'm Jessica Starbuck. I'd like to talk to you about this." Her arm gestured toward the burned barn beside the new one, toward the scattered corral poles.

"What for, what are you going to do about it?" Wertz asked a little truculently. He wasn't happy about having his place burned to the ground.

"I hope to find out who did it and put a stop to it."

"Hicks done it, that's who done it!" Wertz said aggressively. He came forward a step, trembling with anger. "You want to stop it, whoever you are, go stop Grant Hicks."

"Hicks didn't do it," Ki said. "He hired us to find out who did," he added embroidering the facts a little.

"He always wanted to buy me out," Wertz persisted. "He covets my land, covets my good land."

"Maybe so," Jessica said to mollify him a little. "Let me ask you this, though—did you see this done?"

"The burning, no—but I saw him the other time."

"How was he dressed?" Jessie asked.

Wertz, who had opened his mouth to speak, halted momentarily. "Why?" he finally murmured.

"Just wanted to know."

"It was dark," Wertz said defensively.

The boy spoke for the first time. "He was all in shiny armor, wasn't he, Dad?"

"Shut up," the elder Wertz grumbled.

"Well?" Jessie said.

"Well—maybe he was. Who's going to believe it if I say a thing like that?"

"Did the law?" Ki wanted to know.

"The law? Carl Dant? That's a laugh. Why would I report anything to him?" Wertz added, "I take care of my own problems. Out here a man has to."

"When he can. How do you mean to take care of this one?"

Wertz seemed stumped for the first time. He mopped at his forehead and stood watching the mountains for a moment, the breeze cooling his work-heated body. The anger seemed to be draining from him.

"Come on," he invited at last, "I've got cool spring water. Let's set and sip and talk."

They sat and sipped and talked. The story was much the same as Grant Hicks's tale. Wertz hadn't bothered to complain much because he had been laughed at when he did talk about it. Also, he had the notion his neighbor was behind it, though he was at a loss to explain where Grant Hicks could have gotten a suit of armor.

"He hasn't been back," Wertz concluded, "in a week or so. Maybe he's figured out a .44 can go through that funny metal suit—you say Hicks tagged him?"

"He thinks his wife did."

Wertz nodded. "That'll keep him off our backs."

26

Ki rose from his crouch and handed the tin dipper he had been using to Wertz. "Maybe. Maybe they will only use other methods."

"Let 'em try it," Wertz said, regaining his truculence, but there was some doubt in his eyes. "Me and the boy will handle it."

The boy looked even more doubtful. Ki and Jessie swung aboard and rode out, hearing the sawing and hammering before they were out of sight. Whatever Wertz was, he was a worker, and that was a part of what made this dirty. These men had fought Indians a long while ago, fought hard weather, wolves, white raiders, and hard times. Now that they had built something here, the cartel wanted to drive them out.

They reached the third ranch at noon. Al Jankowitz had a different way of handling trouble. He ran for the house at their approach and locked himself in, refusing even to talk, although Jessie and Ki couldn't have looked much like raiding outlaws.

"He was scared silly," Jessica commented as they went on.

"He had the right," Ki said. He nodded to the fresh grave under the oak tree.

They began to see fewer cattle and more corn, more sheep, and finally the Indian village with smoke rising from the cluster of wickiups built along the bluff to the west.

"They are still back there," Ki said at one point. Jessica had nearly forgotten.

"Who? The men trailing us?"

"Yes, and it begins to seem unlikely that we ride this trail by coincidence. They are not Indians."

"Sure of that?" Jessie asked, but if Ki said it, he was sure. He had seen or heard something that confirmed his belief. Hats against the distant skyline, perhaps.

27

They were back there. Stalking.

The Indian village was nearly deserted as they rode into it and past the smoke racks, the tanning hides, the wickiups built in the old manner of mud and poles, watertight, and warm.

The village was deserted, but that was only appearance perhaps. Jessica seemed to feel eyes on her, but turning this way and that she saw no one. She unconsciously touched the butt of the slate-gray .38 revolver she wore.

Ki halted his horse in the middle of the village and waited. After a while an old man came out. He was very tall for a Ute, erect, and white-haired. He looked at Ki, at Jessie, and then nodded his head toward his wickiup.

Jessie looked at Ki and they slid from their mounts, following.

"Sit there and there," the old Ute said as they entered. "A woman cannot sit on the right side."

In the darkness Jessie had trouble making out much of anything, but as she sat and her eyes adjusted she saw the Ute, bare shouldered, sitting and staring back patiently.

"You knew we were coming," she said.

"Yes, of course. These are times of trouble again. We watch."

"Trouble?"

"The trouble. The ghost in the shining suit," the Ute answered and Ki glanced at Jessica.

"That is why we have come," Ki said. "My name is Ki and this is Jessica Starbuck. We are looking for the man in the shining suit."

"He is dead," the Ute said. He lit a long-stemmed clay pipe with a match, which he gazed at in wonder. He hadn't quite gotten used to the new world his people lived in.

"What do you mean?" Jessie asked. "You say the man in armor is dead—did you kill him?"

28

"No."

"But you found him dead?"

"He is a ghost; that is all," the old man said. "A ghost who has come to us. I myself saw him, I, Chi-Tha. I saw him and I knew who he was."

"Who was he?"

"Spanish man. Spanish man in bright armor."

"I don't understand," Jessica said.

Chi-Tha told them. "It was so long ago, before my grandfather's time, but we know it all from a song, a true song. Once the Spanish men came and they wanted to make slaves of us, and they came with bright armor and horses before there were any horses here. They came but we fought back and one night we surprised their camp and took them all away."

The old man rocked back and forth as he puffed gently on his pipe. "In those days it was necessary to hurt the men before they died, you see, so that they would lose their pride and go as cowards into the other land. We would not make warriors of them for our dead to fight. And so we tortured them until one by one they cried like women.

"Then," he said with a slight shrug, "they were killed. But there was one man, a man braver than the others, and no matter what was done he would not cry out with pain. He just cursed us. He cursed the Utes, their fathers, their children, and said, 'I will never die, I will return, and when I do, I will kill you all with famine and plague and blood.'"

Then Chi-Tha seemed to be finished. He could almost have been asleep except that the smoke continued to flow from his lips in small puffs.

To Jessie the Ute's story seemed incomplete. "And now you think he has come?"

Chi-Tha lifted his head with something like astonishment in his eyes. "Of course, white lady! Of course, he has come back, this Spanish man—did he not say he would?"

Ki could see Jessica was going to waste her time trying to talk the old Ute out of this notion and he shook his head, asking instead, "What will happen now, Chi-Tha?"

"Now what happens we do not know. He comes and we know he will one day open his medicine bag and let loose the plague and the blood storm. Then we shall all die."

"If you do not leave," Ki suggested.

"Yes," Chi-Tha said with resignation, "just so. I think then we will leave if he does not leave us alone. The shaman prays and makes smoke, but so far it has done no good. The Spanish curse is too strong."

Trying to talk further to the Ute was like trying to storm the locked door of the frightened Al Jankowitz's house. They gave it up, and as they stepped outside into the cool, clean air, Ki tried to discover something more practical.

"The knight . . . the Spanish ghost. Which way does he ride when he departs, Chi-Tha? Can you tell me that?"

"Toward the sun," the Ute answered with surprise. "Do not the dead always ride toward the place where the sun dies?" He lifted a bony finger and pointed west, toward the hills, toward the town of Camden beyond where, they had been told, something was happening.

Something was happening all right, but what it was Jessie and Ki couldn't guess just then. But they would find out. Death was riding the long valley. The ranchers were scared; the Utes frightened enough to move off their land. Jessica Starbuck had the idea that if they didn't move, and soon, things were going to get worse.

Just a hell of a lot worse.

"Which way?" Ki asked Jessie as they returned to their horses.

Jessica Starbuck lifted her eyes to the hills. "Toward the

30

place where the sun dies, Ki. That's the way he rides; that's the way we ride."

"Toward Camden," Ki pointed out as he swung aboard his sorrel gelding.

"It begins to fit together, doesn't it?"

"Maybe." Ki frowned. "There's something we don't know about this, however, something very important and I'd like to learn it before we step on it."

"And get bitten," Jessie said with a laugh.

"Exactly." Ki wasn't smiling at all. He admired Jessica as no one else could, still she was headstrong, too determined at times. She thought of the cartel to the exclusion of all else, including her own safety.

They rode into the hills where the shadows lay like damp, dark pools. Ki paused at the crest of a low ridge where a single oak tree grew, and he looked back into the White River Basin, his eyes following the course of the river, seeking.

"They're still back there?" Jessica asked.

"I don't see them now."

"Maybe they were Indians. Or hunters. Travelers."

"Maybe. Perhaps now that they know where we are going they do not need to follow us."

They found a seldom used but clearly defined trail and followed it westward. The sun was already behind the tips of the high mountains, spraying the sky with crimson and gold light. The shadows had deepened in the hollows of the hills.

And Jessica Starbuck saw their man.

"Ki!" she said, her voice rising, her finger pointing out the apparition.

"It is him," Ki said. His voice was firm, but even Ki could be shaken at times. Seeing ghosts can do that.

31

It was a knight, black against the sundown sky, riding a ridge above them. As Jessica called out, he stood against the fiery sky, lance uplifted, charger motionless as cold and dark as wrought iron figures.

"Well?" Jessica said in a whisper.

"Get him," Ki said in response and before Jessie could answer he had heeled the sorrel and stretched it out in a dead run toward the ridge a half mile farther on. Jessie was behind him, her little pony nearly as fast as the sorrel.

Ki glanced up to see that the knight was gone, but that wouldn't prevent his being caught. He couldn't ride fast or far dressed like that, with his horse draped in chain mail. Ki was nearly exultant as he urged the sorrel up the dark slope before him. He had the man.

He had him because even if he could ride at speed he wasn't going to go about it quietly. Ki crested the ridge and slowed his sorrel in confusion. The land before them was nearly flat, covered with grass. There were no trees or heavy brush, no stands of rock.

But the knight was gone.

Ki sat listening, watching, unbelieving. Jessica was beside him then, her pony tossing its head, blowing through its nostrils.

"Where . . . ?" Jessica began but Ki shushed her with a glance. Together they sat in the darkness and listened and watched, but there was nothing. Had it been earlier maybe they could have tracked the knight, but the sun was going down and they could do nothing but start on again toward the town of Camden, carrying a weird and somber mood with them.

# Chapter 4

Camden was a series of rectangular, low shapes against the darker hills beyond. Half a dozen lights were lit in the darkness, and on the far side of town torchlight blazed as if they were having a bonfire.

"What would cause people to settle here?" Ki asked. "How can they possibly be supporting themselves?"

"There must be a way It seems lively enough."

"I wonder if they have a boardinghouse or hotel."

"We can ask." She wasn't much in the mood for sleeping out. The long train ride, the tiring stagecoach trip, and the events of the day had left Jessica exhausted. Ki looked fresher than she, but he had to be tired, too. It was no night for sleeping out in the sage with the cold moon shining.

They found the hotel easily. They had a lot of nerve or optimism to call it that, but it would have to do. Two stories, gray wood, with a false front that shuddered when the wind blew—yet it was almost clean inside. There was sawdust on the floor, a few drinking men at round tables scattered around the lobby, and a bald, apparently senile desk clerk.

"We would like two rooms for the night," Ki said.

"How many?" The clerk blinked and fumbled in his pockets for something.

"Two," Ki repeated. The clerk had fallen to staring at Jessica Starbuck and seemed to have forgotten why he was there. A few more minutes of that finally brought them to the crux of the matter, and they were given two keys that fortunately had the number of their rooms stamped on them since the clerk couldn't recall the numbers.

They went upstairs, Ki leading the way. The men below craned their necks to follow Jessie's ascent.

Their rooms were across from each other at the end of an unlighted corridor. The floor under Ki's feet seemed to shiver with each step.

Ki watched Jessica open her door.

"Everything all right?" he asked.

Jessie yawned. "It'll have to be." The bed was iron, painted white and chipped, with a thin blanket, apparently army issue, on it. A window allowed the moon to peer into the room. There were no curtains, rugs, or frills beyond a wash basin and pitcher.

"I'll leave you then. Sleep well, Jessica, but sleep lightly."

"The men who were following us?"

"Them. Besides, if we are getting nearer to the heart of the cartel's scheme someone will know who we are. They have reason to remember us and we don't pass unnoticed."

Leaving Jessie, Ki crossed to his own room, a mirror image of hers, but perhaps a little shabbier. His window faced away from the moon. Ki was drawn by the flames he could see across town, that bonfire they had seen riding in.

"What reason could there be for that?" he asked himself. He stood, hands clasped behind him, staring out at the flames that rose to thirty feet or more. The longer he watched the fire, the more it seemed to attract him.

He glanced toward the door and then, making a sudden decision, he went out, leaving Jessica to sleep.

The lobby was empty but for three bearded, older men playing a card game that seemed to be more an excuse for bickering than anything else.

One asked Ki, "Going out?"

"I thought I might get something to eat."

"No place open but Bully's. The saloon would have sandwiches still."

"Yesterday's," another of the men laughed. Ki thanked them and went out.

He was hungry. But it was the flames that interested him, bothered him. Camden, they had told them, had virtually been a ghost town and now it had come back to life. Why was that? And why was there a fire burning at this time of the night, a fire which reached up and tickled the dark sky with red and gold feathers?

Ki walked the back alleys out of habit, hearing an occasional owl hoot from the front street, the shriek of pleasure or pain of a woman, the crashing of glass from the saloon. Bully's seemed to be a place of local significance. A saloon usually is.

The shadows were deep and Ki moved softly, catlike, past the litter of the town, the empty beer barrels and bottles, the broken crates and garbage, to the head of the alley. He wasn't far from the fire then. It blazed away beyond a dark cluster of towering spruce trees.

Ki walked toward it, his eyes flickering this way and that. Inside the spruce trees it was temporarily cool, dark, silent, but as he emerged he saw the fire, the sweating men, the labor, heard the cursing, saw the exasperation, the anger on the faces of bulky working men.

35

He went nearer.

They had heavy wagons with wheels as high as Ki's head, and on these blocks of stone were being loaded from a pyramidal stack on a huge ramp.

"Here, are you on this job or not," someone challenged.

"Just watching," Ki told the man.

"Sorry. Ned had him a bunch of Orientals. Thought you was one." The man who was breathing hard wiped his forehead with his cuff. It was very cold, but he was sweating profusely.

"It's late to be working," Ki said, watching as a huge winch lowered a block of gray stone onto the wagon, which sagged with the weight.

"Late. Early. We go around the clock here, mister," the workman told him. "Have been for six months."

"Why?" Ki asked. "What is this job?"

"What is it?" the man laughed. "Why, it's building a castle is what it is, mister. It's building a castle. See the number painted on that block. 637A. This here is a castle put together hundreds of years ago in Europe. Now someone bought it, a man named Whitechapel. Sir John Whitechapel. He had this thing taken apart and brought over here by boat. Now we're putting it back together for him. Can you imagine that? The man's got to be mad. But," the man finished with a shrug, "it's work. A day's pay, you know. I got to be going, friend."

He started away but Ki asked, "This castle. Where is it being built?"

"Up there." The man lifted a finger. "Place called Firecliff. You'll see it in daylight. Christ, how could you miss a castle rising up from the mountain peak?"

Then with an exclamation that was both derisive and amused, the man went back to work, shouting something at someone. Ki stood and watched.

He watched and his mind made several connections simultaneously. Between a castle from Europe and a knight riding the dark mountains. Between Sir John Whitechapel and the knight. He looked toward the dark hills, seeing, or thinking he saw by moonlight a craggy unfinished castle against the sky.

With a last glance at the struggling workmen, the creaking winches and blazing firelight, Ki started homeward.

He didn't get far.

They came at him in the spruce trees. He saw nothing of their moon-shadowed faces but that they were white and determined.

"There he is," one with a whispery voice said, "get him," and they lunged at Ki.

They were too close, too fast. Ki couldn't produce or throw *shuriken* in these quarters. Instead, he cried out a warning and began to strike back.

The man on his left had a knife. Ki kicked him on the kneecap and slashed at his nose with his elbow, breaking it. The thug yowled with pain and blood spattered both men.

Moving in a circle, Ki blocked a blow with a *gedanbarai,* a downward block. The man reeled, and as he staggered back, Ki leapt, rising in a *tobi-geri,* a bone shattering kick which sunk into the new attacker's belly, driving him away with a grunt as the wind was driven from his body.

Ki landed, crouched, and blocked the downward blow of a club with crossed wrists before he grabbed the thug's shirtfront and pulled him off balance, tripping him as he went by, chopping with the flat of his hand at his neck just below the ear, stunning the bundle of nerves there, paralyzing the muscles so that the man fell to the dark earth and lay twitching, his mind sending out messages that the numbed muscles could not respond to.

Ki was suddenly alone. He held his arms upraised de-

37

fensively, turning slowly, searching the darkness of the grove. But they were down, these three, groaning and writhing, and there were no others.

Quickly he searched their bodies, but there was nothing in their pockets. They had been ineffective but not careless. Ki rose, wiped back his hair, took a deep breath of the cold mountain air and started back toward the hotel.

Jessie's head came up. There was someone, something in the corridor and her hand groped for the .38 Colt beneath her pillow.

It's nothing, she thought, only Ki.

Of course, it was Ki. She rose and slipped from the bed. She was naked in the night and the moon glossed her body with liquid gold. The tap at the door slowed her for a moment, caused her hand to tighten on the butt of the Colt.

"Who is it?" she asked in a whisper, leaning toward the door.

There was no answer. Jessie moved nearer, putting her ear to the door. The air was cool. Her nipples stood taut.

"Who's there? Ki?"

"Yes, me," the voice responded and with a little sigh of relief, she lowered her pistol and unlocked the door.

The tumblers clicked free and the door was kicked in. The Colt clattered to the floor as two big men barged into the room, dark and malicious, smelling of whiskey.

"That's her, all right," one voice said.

The other man had Jessie by the arms and he was near to her, his body against her naked flesh.

"That's her; let's do it," the other man said nervously.

"What's the hurry?" the man holding her asked. His callused hand slipped to Jessica's breast and caressed the nipple. She kicked out savagely, her bare heel catching his ankle, but the man just laughed.

38

Jessica tried desperately to twist free, throwing her knee at the intruder's groin, but she was virtually helpless as he held her wrists in one massive hand.

"Ki!" she called out, but there was no response from the room across the corridor. "Ki! I need you."

"You don't need anybody, sister. No one but Jack Crater," the big man sneered and he shoved her toward her bed where she landed, sprawled, kicking out at the thug as he unbuttoned his trousers with one hand.

"Jack," the other man hissed, "they sent us to *kill* her!"

"There's time for that, but I'm not going to waste something prime like this."

"Jack—" the other one pleaded.

"Shut up. Watch the door. The Chinaman's around somewhere."

But he wasn't. Ki wasn't in the hotel.

Jack dropped his trousers and lurched forward, his hairy weight falling against Jessica Starbuck who wasn't ready to give up yet. Stiffened fingers jabbed at the man's eyes, and she chopped at his throat with the side of her hand. Jack fought her off. He had a hundred pounds on her and that helped. He lay pressed against Jessie who thrashed from side to side. He figured to get a few cheap thrills before he got to the bigger thrill of murdering a young woman.

It didn't work that way.

The man at the door heard a soft footstep and turned. He was too slow. The long dark stiletto lifted through abdominal muscle and the black point touched heart and lungs. The man who had tried to make money through murder found that death doesn't pay a cent.

He slumped to the floor and the big man on the bed turned with a growl, his hand reaching for his gunbelt. His pants were around his ankles, however, and before he could snatch his Remington double-action from its holster, the dark figure had crossed the room and ripped upward with his stiletto, opening Jack's throat. Hot blood gushed from the narrow wound and the thug rolled away to die on the floor, strangling.

Jessica Starbuck watched the man fall, watched him die, and then she came from the bed to throw herself into the survivor's arms.

"Oh, Ki! You came just in time."

And he held her, his hand going up and down her naked back, following her spine from the base of her neck to the cleft of her ass, his finger lingering there as he drew her nearer, flattening her breasts against his chest.

"You're not Ki!"

There wasn't much doubt of that. The stranger had begun to harden against her, had begun to arouse in Jessie deep, liquid longings.

"No," the stranger's voice said.

Still, she didn't pull away from him immediately. Still, she let his hand rest on her buttock, feeling the smooth cool flesh, the strength beneath the skin. Still, she felt his breath on her cheek before shaking free of the inexplicable feeling of need. She stepped away and snatched her blouse up.

"Who are you? Who are these men?" Jessie asked out of the darkness. "Where is Ki?"

The dark man, the intruder, the man who had saved her, seemed to be able to penetrate the darkness with his eyes. Jessie could feel his gaze on her and it was a thrilling, warm feeling.

"I don't know where this Ki is," he said at last in a polished baritone that seemed to have a British accent. "I only saw these men intrude. I came to assist you."

"How could you have seen them? Who are you?"

There were footsteps in the corridor outside now, and by

40

the moonlight Jessie saw the dark man turn that way. "I must go," he said.

"But you haven't answered my questions," Jessica said.

"And I can't—not now."

The footsteps were nearer, so he went to her and kissed her deeply. She relaxed briefly in his arms, feeling the power of his kiss, of his male body. Then he brushed her forehead with his lips and he was gone. Crossing to the window, he stepped out into the night and vanished.

The door burst open; Ki rushed in.

"Jessie?"

"I'm all right, Ki."

"What's happened here?"

She told him, "I'm not sure. I'm really not sure." Jessica could still feel the warmth, the hardness of the intruder's body against her flesh, feel his searching hands and hungry mouth. She realized suddenly that she was still naked and ther were dead men on her floor.

Snatching up her blouse and jeans, she told Ki about it as she dressed.

"These," Ki said, crouching over the dead, "I understand. Hired killers. But the other one—who was he?" He looked to the window where the dark man had gone. Crossing to it, he looked down, seeing nothing in the night. It was an easy step out to the ledge and then a drop to the ground.

"Whoever he was, it's a good thing he showed up when he did," Jessica said, turning up the lamp.

"But you see, don't you, Jessica—that is the very strange part about it."

She was rapidly brushing her hair before the faded, chipped mirror on the back of the door. She turned to glance at Ki.

"What do you mean?"

41

"Who was he, Jessica? What was he doing here?"

"Why, I assumed he was a hotel guest who happened to be passing the room."

"And then leaped from the window instead of staying behind?"

"Maybe he is a wanted man, a married man," Jessie replied, putting her hat on. They had agreed without discussing it to get out of the hotel. One chance was enough to give the cartel men.

"Maybe. Maybe, too, he was watching you, Jessie."

"Watching me? Why?" Her eyebrows drew together quizzically.

"I don't know. But I feel this was no passing stranger—and look at the way he killed," Ki pointed out. "Skillful, very skillful indeed, for a man who has not learned his trade where death is a specialty."

"Ready?" Jessica asked, shouldering into her jacket and picking up her bedroll.

"Now you are ready to sleep out in the sage beneath the cold moon."

"You bet," she answered. "I'd rather wake up cold than sleep warm—sleep and sleep."

"So would I. I'll get my things."

They went out, leaving the befuddled clerk their keys and two dollars. Outside it was cool, and they almost regretted their decision.

"We have learned something, Jessie. They definitely know we are here."

"The cartel?"

"That's right." They crossed the street toward the stable. There was frost on the rutted road, noise still emanating from the saloon. "Attacking me was not proof, attacking us both in the same night is conclusive as far as I'm concerned. We—"

42

"Wait, Ki, you didn't tell me you were attacked." She stopped and took his arm, half turning him, the moonlight showing the concern in her eyes. She knew Ki and all of his strengths, but she didn't believe him invisible. No man is, and one day it would be his blood soaking into the ground perhaps.

"It was nothing, really. Yes, I was attacked. I think it must have been the men we saw following us from Sharpsville."

They started on again and Ki told her what he had discovered. "And so," he concluded, "we now have a knight and a castle. Where would a logical person look for our dark knight?"

"Where else?" Jessica lifted her eyes to the hills, seeing or imagining she saw the stark form of a walled castle. To the north of town the bonfire still burned.

Inside the stable they saddled up silently by the light of a kerosene lantern. "I know you're going to explain all of this to me, Ki," Jessica said at last as she kneed her balky pony to force it to expel the extra air it was holding, tightened her cinch, and then swung aboard.

"I am," Ki said, "as soon as I understand it myself. There is a touch of madness in the air and it disturbs me."

"Ghosts?" Jessie teased. "Spanish curses?"

Ki's reply was soft and serious. "Perhaps. Perhaps that, Jessica."

# Chapter 5

Jessica Starbuck awoke stiff and cold. The country around her was rife with flowering purple sage where butcher birds and thrushes hopped and complained. The sun was golden, flooding the hills with color as it left the White River Basin in deep shadow.

Jessie groaned and sat up. It had been a nearly sleepless night, and when she had managed to fall off near dawn, blanket tugged over her head, she had begun to dream of dark knights who came to her naked in the night, taking her down into a bed of grass.

Her sleep wasn't real restful.

Ki looked alert and rested but then he was far superior at meditation, at convincing his body that all was well, that it was warm, the ground soft.

Jessie rolled out and began to pick up.

Ki stood watching, the wind shifting his dark, straight hair. "Did you want to go to town to eat?" he asked.

45

"No, I don't have that kind of patience, do you?"

"No, not this morning."

"I want to see this castle, Ki. I want to see it and I want to see the men who are building it. I want to see this dark knight, if that's where he comes from."

"And your young savior?" Ki asked.

"Who?"

"Your man from last night—don't you want to see him again?"

Jessie started to deny that automatically, but she thought of the press of the man against her, of the sudden thrill spreading across her loins, and she smiled. "Maybe. If he's there, maybe."

They rode out westward again and Jessie began to be sorry she hadn't been patient enough to go into town to eat. Her stomach complained constantly as they rode.

The sun rose higher and the shadows disappeared. The hills began to be forested. Pine and cedar trees grew in deep ranks, flooding the mountain slopes. There were wild-flowers in the meadows and plenty of game.

They entered a deep wood and rode silently for five miles or more, the sun shafting through the trees to stain the earth with gold.

When they emerged from the wood, they were looking up at the castle.

"Yes," Ki said with satisfaction, a small hiss escaping his lips. They held up their horses and sat, staring.

A bit of Europe had been carried across the sea, across America, to be set up piece by piece on a mountain crag. Atop a gray crumbling ledge, three to four hundred feet up, a gray castle rose. It seemed to be nearly completed, with battlements and towers as solid as those thrown up by medieval lords hundreds of years ago. A red pennant flew from a pole atop one tower.

46

"Madness," Ki said under his breath, but Jessie heard him.

"You don't like this much, do you, Ki?"

He turned toward her. "Do you?"

She just smiled. "Let's have a closer look."

They wound through the forest for many miles, circling northward, searching for a way up to the castle. From their present position it seemed impossible, as if the knight or king or madman who owned the place had found an impregnable position to hold off hordes.

"The workmen are getting up somehow," Ki said and eventually they found the way. From the west a long, wedge-shaped valley opened to a higher plain, which seemed to have been burned over recently. The plain ran to the edge of the sheer precipice where the great anachronism, the castle, stood like a sentinel against a deep blue Colordo sky.

Wagons rolled toward the castle. Shirtless, red-faced men sat on the tailgates behind huge blocks of gray granite, sacks of mortar, ironwork, and crates.

The castle, which had seemed dreamlike, grew large and solid and formidable as Jessica and Ki rode toward it.

"A drawbridge," Jessie said, half amused, half astonished.

And there was one, made of heavy planks, new ones, bound together with iron straps, drawn by chains that ran up past the portcullis. She glanced at Ki, hoping to see a smile on his face, but there was still that worried look, the one that said madness.

They passed through the gates of the castle unnoticed among the workmen who seemed to be going in all directions at once and into the courtyard of the great structure.

"And now," Ki said, "I want to find this Sir John White-chapel."

A cowboy, incongruous in his wide hat and red bandanna,

47

leather chaps, and crooked smile, led a string of three huge horses past Ki and Jessica. The shoulder of the near horse came above the head of Jessie's pony.

"They look like draft horses," she said, twisting around to watch them plod on.

Ki told her, "It takes a lot of horse to carry a man in armor."

"Yes, I suppose it does," she answered thoughtfully.

They found their way to a great oaken door, which stood open to the world. A man with a slaughtered hog on his back was passing them, entering the house.

"Where is Whitechapel?" Ki asked.

"Up there, I reckon," the butcher answered. He lifted his chin toward the stony upper apartments. "He normally is this time of day—having a little wine for lunch."

The man winked and went on and Jessie and Ki swung down from their horses.

"It's not really an ominous atmosphere," Jessie said. "Men working. Building. These aren't cartel people."

"No," Ki agreed, *these* are not cartel people."

About Sir John Whitechapel he had reservations yet. The cartel had its base in Europe, and though it seemed to be headed by Prussians, they had on other occasions encountered cartel operatives from a variety of European nations.

They went into a corridor alive with activity, clotted with stone dust, heavy with American curses, and walked on. An inner room seemed complete. A long oaken table ran nearly the considerable length of the room. Thirty people could have seated themselves at that table. In the alcoves above and along the walls, flags were hung.

"You there!" A voice called from the upper gallery and they looked that way. "You—looking for the kitchen?"

The man Ki finally picked out was spare with white hair and a mustache and wearing tweeds. He leaned out expectantly from the second story gallery.

"No, sir. We are looking for Sir John Whitechapel."

"Kitchen help? Splendid looking lady!"

"No, not kitchen help," Ki answered.

The Englishman looked crestfallen. "Well, then, come up, won't you? I'm Whitechapel."

They had to poke around a little until they found the gray stone steps spiraling upwards. Ki led the way, and when they emerged, Whitechapel was there, waiting. He had tugged on a cap and placed a monocle in front of his blue right eye.

"Hoped you were the pastry people. How far is it to San Francisco anyway? Wrote a month ago, a full month. Damned country has no right to be so large."

"Sir Whitechapel . . ." Ki began. The old Englishman was looking at Jessica however.

"Splendid looking lady! And what did I call you up for?" he asked.

Jessie smiled. "You didn't call us up, Sir Whitechapel. We are here on business, rather dreary business. My name is Jessica Starbuck and this is Ki. We—"

"Starbuck? Starbuck—you can't be related to Alex Starbuck! Well, perhaps you are—look at you." His hands held her face briefly. He sighed distantly. "Much like *her*. Your mother. I see it now—you are Alex's daughter, aren't you?"

"Yes. Yes, I am."

"Thought so, yes." The old man was briefly lost in reminiscences. "Come along, come along," he said as someone called for him from a higher level of the castle. Jessie and Ki tagged after him as they climbed another flight of ancient stairs and emerged on to an outer balcony, a half circle clinging to the side of a gray tower.

"What is it, then?" Sir Whitechapel called down.

An American in a flop hat and faded red undershirt called

up, "That you, Whitechapel? None of us knows what to do with this dingus you got here. Where's it go?"

"Dingus? *Dingus!*" Whitechapel became indignant. "That dingus as you call it is my ballista. Thirteenth Century. Destroyed the Earl of Craddock's keep during a siege."

The workman looked dubious or simply uncomprehending. "Yeh, okay. Where do you want the damn thing?"

Whitechapel seemed ready to vault the stone parapet and leap to the courtyard below. The device, which looked to Jessie like a great portable catapult of ancient design, was sitting in the middle of the court. There were eight horses hitched to the war machine.

"Find Sir Ethelbert. He'll direct you. Find my brother!"

"All right, boss," the American said and Whitechapel turned away. His face was red—with anger Jessica first supposed, and as he began to move his shoulders convulsively, she thought he was having a fit of apoplexy, but the shaking ended in a loud gust of laughter.

He laughed so hard that he had to lean against the wall to support himself. "Excellent," the white-headed nobleman said when he was able to speak. "These colonials!—Whitechapel, where do you want this damned dingus?—Excellent!"

Jessie and Ki smiled politely but they couldn't share the Englishman's pleasure.

"There is something serious on your minds," the old man said, sobering.

"Very serious."

"Well, then, let's discuss it. I've been doing nothing but enjoying myself since I began this project. I forget at times that there is still a real world and its troubles beyond my castle walls. Follow me, please."

They reentered the castle and swept down a long, bleak corridor past shields and suits of armor, small alcoves where wooden chairs or icons sat silently, and into a fairly well-lighted apartment where everything was old, musty, out of time.

"My chamber," Whitechapel said.

He had tapestries on the walls, three wooden chairs around a table set with candelabra, a four-poster bed with a spread that bore a heraldic emblem. Six narrow windows allowed the sunlight to pierce the thick stone walls.

"You see, the past can be kept alive. Very expensive, I admit," the lord of the castle said, "but then I can afford it. I learned my trade—merchantman—from a man who was the best, Alex Starbuck."

"You knew my father."

"Very well. Very well, indeed. We ran indigo together once, and then for a time it was silk. Of course, Alex Starbuck had many other interests at the same time. While he was becoming monumentally rich, I was merely . . . vastly wealthy," Whitechapel finished with another chuckle. "And a good part of that due to Alex Starbuck's guidance, I must say. Yes, I knew him well."

"You're retired now, I take it," Jessica said. Whitechapel had found a decanter of brandy and he offered them each a glass. Both refused and he poured himself a tall drink.

"Retired, yes, quite right," Whitechapel said. He removed his monocle and let it hang around his neck on its silk ribbon. "Retired and living, damn all! For the first time I am thinking about something besides how much I was losing on the one hand, gaining on the other."

"But this—" Jessie said. She made a gesture that encompassed the entire castle. "This is where you have chosen to live?"

"It is my dream. It is where I must live."

"In a castle?" Ki asked.

"Yes, of course, sir. You wouldn't understand unless you

51

knew me better. My life has been one of commerce, my outer life, but I have always longed for another life, another time—for one gone by. I am a knight of the realm, sir. Yes, an authentic English knight—but what does that signify today in this modern world of gunpowder and nationalism? Where is the past? Is it not mocked?

"In the days I would have preferred to live in, I should have been lord of my castle, owner of all I surveyed. I should have gone forth to battle with pageantry and spectacle, with the good wishes of my subjects, with squires in attendance and my good men beside me. There would have been maidens in need of rescue in those times, my friends, and deeds of gallantry, who knows—perhaps a dragon deep in the black forest..."

Ki and Jessie looked at one another. The old man went on for a time more, recreating in his mind the world he might have inhabited once, long ago.

"And so," Whitechapel said, putting his glass down on the table, "I have decided to do what few men can do. I have decided to go back into the past, to remake it. I have made a life's study of chivalry and medieval life. I am determined, after living most of my years in a way which pleased the world, to finish my life in a way that most pleases me. Here, far from the corrupting influences of modern civilization, I shall raise a medieval town. I shall become what I have always dreamed of being, a feudal lord. This, my friends, is why you see this castle standing so far from its origin, why I have come to the American West."

"Father—" the door to the room opened and a tall man in a dark suit stood there. He was handsome, his features sharply chiseled, his dark hair swept back, a gold chain across the front of his vest. "I'm sorry," he apologized, "I didn't know we had guests."

"Come in, Reginald. Please. This is Jessica Starbuck—

52

you've heard me mention her father—and her friend."

"Starbuck?" the young man said and he didn't need to say more. It was him, the one with the stiletto. His eyes smiled at Jessica and drifted to Ki.

"You recall me speaking of him, surely," Whitechapel insisted. "This, Miss Starbuck, is Reginald Whitechapel, heir to the castle."

The old man chuckled a little and Jessie glanced at Reggie Whitechapel, expecting to see tolerant amusement in his eyes. There was nothing of the sort there. The expression was dark, unreadable.

But Jessie wondered. She wondered how it felt to know that your father was going to take the money you should have inherited and build himself a castle in America. If Reginald felt rancor he was good at concealing it.

"I would think," Ki ventured, "that you would take your time in the building, enjoying each phase of it."

"I've always been an impatient man," Whitechapel replied. "I haven't got a lot of time left on this earth. Besides, if the tournament is going to be held on schedule we have to complete the work quickly."

"Tournament?" Jessie inquired.

"Oh, yes, absolutely! If one's going to recreate medieval life, why there must be a jousting tourney. The fair first, of course, for the local peasants. Then the tournament."

"Father is not alone in his eccentricities," Reginald said. His eyes—dark, probing eyes—remained on Jessica and she could feel his want.

"No, not at all," Whitechapel said. "There are men such as myself all around the world, chiefly in Europe, of course, but some in South America, one prominent lord in Japan."

"All of you medievalists."

"Yes, of course. That is the only time to have lived, *to* live. Jousting tournaments are held every two years in various countries. This is the first time I shall be able to host one of my own, of course, and so I'm anxious that everything goes well."

"Armored knights," Ki said, "from around the world. There will be combat among them and presumably an award to the victor."

"Yes, quite right. And we have some excellent horsemen among us, men who have studied the broadsword or the mace, who are expert with the lance. Some, I daresay, who could have their own with the knights of old."

Ki asked, "Each of you has his champion then?"

"Oh, quite right." Whitechapel had decided to pour himself another brandy. "We old lords can't be expected to enter the lists, I'm afraid. Each of us has a champion, a skilled fighter."

"And may I ask who your champion is, Sir Whitechapel?" Jessica said.

The white haired man blinked, "Why, of course—it's my son, Reginald. Reggie is our champion and as skilled a combatant as any you'll find."

Reggie's expression hadn't changed. He watched Jessica and she watched back, feeling the pull of him, the male attraction. She watched him and his eyes never wavered. She could recall the kiss of the night before vividly—she could recall the stiletto killing quietly, efficiently.

"You must stay, of course," Sir Whitechapel said briskly. "Stay for the tournament and the fair . . . I say, did we ever get around to discussing just what your business in this isolated part of the country is?"

"No," Jessica replied, "we didn't. We're only traveling, Sir Whitechapel, seeing the country, you know."

"Why then you shall be able to stay," he said cheerfully. "Unless you have a schedule."

"We'd be delighted," Jessica answered. Reggie's eyes

flickered a little then. Ki's expression hardened a little. "Ki and I are most interested in seeing your tournament, in watching your champion do battle."

Sir Whitechapel sensed something in Jessica's tone, something that seemed to put him briefly on guard, but he shrugged it off.

"Fine. Very well, then. Reginald, see if you can't find a chambermaid—bell pulls aren't in yet—and arrange a comfortable room for each of our guests. We're delighted to have you with us. We shall try to make your visit a most interesting one, shall we not, Reggie?"

"We'll do our very best," the dark man said, "to make it as interesting as possible."

# Chapter 6

"He's mad," she said.

The maid's name was Carrie. She was all of twenty, pert, and had dark hair and blue eyes. She was all dumplings and apple cheeks with firm, round breasts that were pale and freckled where they showed above the white maid's blouse she wore. A white lacy cap was pinned to the back of her head. She wore a black skirt and carried a bundle of linen as she kneed open the door to Ki's room.

"Sir Whitechapel," Ki said, holding the heavy oaken door as she bounced into the room and tossed the linen on to Ki's bed.

"That's right. Mad as a hatter. I'd keep my door locked at night, if I was you. I always do, that's for sure. Around here, Lawd!"

"You don't really believe his madness is dangerous, do you? It seems a harmless diversion."

"Yeah?—Tall, aren't you," she said to Ki. "How tall exactly?"

She stood coyly before Ki and he had a magnificent view of her breasts. Her blue eyes sparkled as she saw his eyes on her.

"Like them?" she asked. Ki decided to return to the safer topic.

"Why did you come out here if you're frightened of Sir Whitechapel?"

Carrie made up his bed as they spoke. From time to time she paused in a way that let Ki have a good study of her rounded, nicely shaped rear end.

"Oh, well, first off he ain't done anything, you know. It's just that a person gets these feeling, you see. As to why I came, why he pays well. Got me a bonus and a trip to America, and if I don't like it one day, I can pack up and get out, can't I? Though what I'd do in this country if I left, I don't know. Need someone, do you?" she asked saucily.

"Not permanently, no."

"Doesn't have to be permanent, you know," she said.

She had finished the bed, after shaking out a pillow and stuffing it in a clean case.

"I'd really be interested in what does go on around here," Ki said. "Besides the building, I mean."

"Not much, I suppose—if you don't count the spooks and spectres."

"The what?"

Carrie sat on the bed, bouncing on it a few times, her skirt lifted and tucked between her thighs. She patted the bed beside her.

"Sit here. You ain't stuffy, are you? You're common folk like me; everyone in this country is, they say."

Ki sat beside her and Carrie's hand immediately found

58

his thigh, resting there as they spoke.

"Spooks and spectres," Ki prompted. "What about them?"

"Well, they come with the castle, don't they? The eighth duke of what not and the seventh earl's lady and all that—the place has got to have ghosts."

"Does it?"

"Does it have ghosts?" Her blue eyes were wide and frank. Briefly they turned away from Ki's. Her hand squeezed his thigh and it seemed to be an involuntary gesture.

"That's what I want to know, Carrie. Does it have ghosts."

"I seen them," she said softly, her eyes returning to his dark, thoughtful eyes.

"Yes?"

"That's all," Carrie said. "Why don't you sneak us a kiss, Mr. Ki?" She scooted nearer and it didn't seem like a bad idea at all, but Ki refrained for the time being.

"What do they look like, these ghosts?" he asked. Carrie sat up straighter, pouting a little with disgust.

"Like castle ghosts should look. Men in armor, you know."

"In the middle of the night?"

"Course! When else do they walk the castle?"

"And ride away," Ki said.

"How did you know that?" Carrie asked, her wide blue eyes growing wider yet.

"It is true, isn't it?"

"Yes," she said, speaking almost in a whisper, leaning nearer to Ki. "I seen him, this one ride out nearly every night. All in black armor and carrying a lance. Eerie, it is, Mr. Ki."

The door now opened completely with a thunderous bang. A big man with square cut red hair and huge shoulders stood there. Ki came to his feet automatically.

"You, girl!" the man bellowed. "What are you doing here? Get out."

59

"Yes, sir, yes," Carrie said, fear evident in her blue eyes.

"And just who the hell are you?" the man asked Ki truculently.

"I am a guest of Sir Whitechapel," Ki said in an even voice, watching as Carrie scooted past the man, her head below his shoulder.

"Yes? Not that Japanese knight, are you?" The man squinted with curiosity.

"No, not a Japanese knight."

"Don't know what the hell we need more people around here for," the redhead said, and then without another word he turned and stalked off, leaving a bemused Ki to clean up and contemplate what he had learned of spooks, spectres, and knights.

"That is Ethelbert," Reginald Whitechapel said to Jessica Starbuck. She turned to see a redheaded man striding away from Ki's room, which was farther down the long corridor from hers. Reggie stood and watched him go.

"Who is Ethelbert?" Jessie asked.

"My uncle. Stepuncle, actually. He's ill-tempered and bitter." Reginald Whitechapel grinned. "I think it's his name that does it. There's a theory that people are formed partly by their names. Do you hold with that?"

"I don't know."

"You, for example," Reggie said, putting the flat of his hand against the wall where Jessie was leaning. "Jessica. A lovely name. Would you have been so charming, so sure of yourself, so graceful if you'd been named Gertrude? I wonder."

He was nearer yet and Jessie said softly, "Show me the countryside; show me your father's lands."

"Certainly. Meet me in five minutes in the courtyard?"

"That'll be fine," she said, and if she were going to say

60

more, she never had the chance. Reggie's mouth found hers and he kissed her quickly. Then, grinning, he strode off and Jessie watched him.

"You're a dangerous man, I think, Reginald Whitechapel. Very dangerous," Jessie said softly.

She found Ki standing at his window, and she told him what she intended to do.

"I want to look around the countryside and see if anything else is going on out there. If the cartel is ready to move in and take over, there might be signs of their activity."

"And other thugs—they'll be growing impatient with this business of trying to frighten the Indians off."

"Perhaps, but as long as they do it that way the Indians will probably remain quiet. They won't fight back. A gang of armed men would meet plenty of resistance."

"Probably, but the cartel only has so much patience. When they want something, they take it. They won't mind using force if they have to. They won't mind blood."

"No." Jessica Starbuck knew that. The cartel had left a trail of blood behind it.

"Be careful, Jessica."

"I will. Reggie will be with me."

Ki lifted one eyebrow. "You trust him?"

"We'll see," she said cautiously. "For now, yes. What about this Ethelbert? What did he want?"

"A redhead with big shoulders? *Ethelbert?* I'm not sure what he wanted, perhaps only to have a look at me. Perhaps to scold the help. I'll try to find out something about him."

"Apparently he's sir John's stepbrother. Where does that leave him for money? I wonder. Why the devil would he follow Sir John to America?"

"I'll ask around. I have contacts now," Ki said.

*"Yes?"*

"I make friends very easily," Ki said lightly.

61

"And enemies easily as well. Watch yourself, Ki. I don't know what's going on around here yet, but whatever it is, they don't want our noses in it."

No, they didn't want them poking around, and if the cartel were actually behind this, if they knew who Jessie and Ki were, they would do almost anything to see that they never interfered in cartel business again.

Jessie walked the long corridor and went down the unfinished stone steps to the great hall where workmen were lugging in huge crates.

Outside it was cool, bright, breezy. Reggie was waiting with two horses.

"Ready?" he asked, handing her the reins.

"Let's go."

She swung aboard and they rode out of the castle, across the drawbridge, which rattled beneath their horses' hooves, and back into the real world.

A mile on Jessie stopped and looked back. She just looked, shook her head, and started the horse on again. Reggie was watching her. "I know," he said. "Unreality. Madness, eccentricity."

"Why did you come with him?"

Reggie shrugged. "He's my father. I could have stayed in England but this seemed more adventurous."

"You'll inherit the castle one day, I suppose."

"It seems so. And what will I do with it then? Live out my own days as a medieval knight?"

Jessie nodded. "I was wondering how it feels to see the family fortune sunk into something like this."

Reggie said tersely, "He made it; he can spend it."

They rode silently for a while, across the long valley and eastward into the pines. They emerged from the forest to overlook the White River Basin.

"Is that your property, too?" Jessie asked. Reggie wagged his head.

"Indian land."

"It looks like good cattle land. Thousands and thousands of acres of it."

"Maybe. I'm not a cattleman, nor is father. It doesn't interest me in the least and it wouldn't interest him. Nothing outside of the castle walls does."

"And Ethelbert?"

"I don't know what Ethelbert's interested in. I never met the man until this year. He's the black sheep in the family, it seems. He was off somewhere, trying apparently to match my father's success in trade. It doesn't seem to have worked."

Reggie swung down from his horse and walked to Jessie who sat on the little gray pony he had gotten her. His hand rested on her thigh as he looked up at her.

"Get down. Let's walk."

"All right."

"I want to show you something."

Jessie swung a leg over and ground hitched the horse, which was content to crop grass there in the shadow of the pines. Reggie took Jessie's hand and kept it, squeezing it tightly. He led her along the forest path and she followed.

They walked a winding path through moss-covered, gray stones. A tiny stream sheeted over a granite ledge, forming a paper-thin waterfall.

The cabin was among the fern and pine trees.

"Is this it?" she asked. "What you wanted to show me?"

"Yes. Come on."

Still holding her hand, he led her to the stone cabin, opened the door, and took her in. "They tell me an old trapper built it. There couldn't have been anyone but Utes within a hundred miles when he did."

63

Reggie opened the heavy wooden shutters on a window and bluish light poured in. By the light Jessica saw the charcoal sketches and an unfinished painting.

"You're an artist!"

"A dilettante with aspirations. I try."

He watched as she studied the charcoal sketches of wildlife, birds and deer, and the fern in the area. The painting was different.

It sat on an easel and was done in dark cobalt blues and deep grays—ominous colors. It was a dark knight on a dark charger riding before the moon.

"That's nothing," he said quickly. "A failure."

"A self-portrait?" Jessie asked.

Reggie smiled faintly. He didn't answer. Instead, he stepped to her and unbuttoned the top button on her blouse, his lips lowering to kiss her there, to smell the soft scent of her, her womanhood, to feel the pulsing of her blood. He felt her hand on his head, her thumb brushing his ear, and he opened another button, his lips finding her cleavage, soft, secret warm.

There was a bed with a quilt in the corner and Reggie led her to it. Jessie sat on the bed and then lay back and Reggie continued to undress her.

He opened her blouse still more and her ripe, pink-tipped breasts came free to draw forth his hungry eyes, his lips, and hands.

Jessie finished slipping from the blouse by herself; then she wriggled from her skirt as Reggie stepped from his trousers and stood over her, watching the sunlight gloss and shadow her body, watching her eyes light with eagerness.

He went to his knees as she lay back on the bed, and he kissed her inner thighs, working his way upward.

Jessie felt the tingling in her thighs become a hunger as the man slowly, patiently touched his lips to her soft inner

64

flesh. He lifted his head and smiled at her, lifting himself so that he could again give his attention to her taut, pink nipples.

Jessie held his head gently, feeling the rising sensation in her crotch, feeling his maleness pressed against her, the heat and throb of it as Reggie kissed her breasts, then let his lips travel to her throat. Jessica's head lolled back.

He went to his knees again and sat touching her, his fingers probing, gently stimulating, until Jessica slid from the bed her knees spread. Facing Reggie on the floor, she reached for his erect shaft and placed the head of it inside her, holding it there for a long tantalizing minute. Then with her parted lips greedily finding his, she slid onto it, sinking to the depths, shuddering.

Jessie kissed his neck, his ears, his chest, as his hands clenched her buttocks, drifted up her back, held her to him. Reggie began to sway against her and Jessie smiled with pleasure, sighing eager sounds.

She reached between her legs and touched Reggie, feeling the thickness of him. Her fingers stroked Reggie gently and that combined with the sweet warm softness that enveloped him brought him to a hard, sudden climax.

Jessie closed her eyes, feeling his trembling, the pulsing of him, the sudden jerky movement as he clung to her shoulders, pressing his body to hers. Her own body reacted with a swift completion.

Her breathing became rapid, her skin flushed. Her body became soft and damp and she clung to Reggie as lights began to burst inside her skull and wave after wave of sensation swept through her.

It was good, very good, and when Reggie rose, still holding her, and placed her back on the bed, she fell off to sleep, his warm breathing against her throat, his hard body pressed to hers.

It was nearly dusk when she awoke, stretched, smiled at the sleeping man, and said, "All right. Let's get up."

"Stay here," Reggie murmured from out of his half sleep.

"Can't do that. We've got to get back to the castle."

"The hell with that damned castle! Who needs it? I've got all I want here in the cabin."

"You really don't care about money, do you?" Jessie asked, trying to believe him. After all, if Reggie were the sort who could be content with charcoal and paper, a hermit's cabin, he wasn't going to be interested in any cartel offer to make him rich.

"You're right," he said, rolling away from her without answering. "It is getting late."

He rose, dressed silently, and waited at the door for Jessica. He stood looking down the hill toward the valley beyond, toward the White River Basin. He turned toward her slightly as she approached, and in silhouette she was startled to see how much he resembled the dark knight in the painting.

"Ready?" he asked without looking at her. From somewhere beyond she could hear the waterfall trickling. He turned toward Jessie suddenly, half smiling. He walked to her and put his arms on her shoulders and kissed her. There was something lacking in that kiss, however. He was distant suddenly, mysterious.

"Yes, let's go."

The first stars were winking. Far away they could see a bonfire. They would work through the night again in Camden. There was a mad rush to get the castle completed before the fair and jousting tournament.

"Do people get hurt in the tournaments you have?" Jessie asked.

"Men have been killed. Very few do anything about it. They figure if a bunch of grown men want to swing maces at each other, let them. It wasn't so in England—there the police broke up a tournament once. That's one reason my father wanted to leave the country."

Jessie looked up at him as they walked. He was somber, his voice uninflected. His jaw was clenched. They stopped before they got to the horses. Around them the dark pines loomed.

"Jessie," Reginald said, "listen to me. This is no place for you. I want you to leave."

"I can't. Not just yet."

"There's going to be trouble," he said urgently.

She nodded. "I know it. Ki and I have handled trouble before. You might be surprised."

"I might be at that," he said quietly. He had been holding her shoulders. Now his hands fell away. "But I wish you would leave. There's something unhealthy going on here. Can't you sense it, Jessica?"

"I can sense it, yes. That's why I'm here." She paused, looking into his eyes. "What is it, Reggie? What exactly do you think is wrong here?"

"Madness," he said and the word echoed in Jessie's mind. Wasn't that what Ki had felt all along, madness?

"Who is mad? What is it, Reggie. Tell me."

"Maybe," he said, lifting his eyes, "it is me."

And then he took her arm painfully and flung her aside so that Jessica Starbuck was thrown to the earth as Reggie Whitechapel roared.

# Chapter 7

Jessica was flung to the ground. She rolled over and reached for her .38, not finding it before Reggie roared out something unintelligible and guns fired from the trees.

Crimson tongues of flame spat danger at Jessica and Reggie. The Englishman hurled himself toward Jessie and the two of them scrambled for cover. Bullets from unseen guns cut at the trees, spattering bark.

Jessie, on one knee now, had found her Colt and she waited patiently until she saw a muzzle flash from across the clearing.

When she saw it, she fired rapidly, three times squeezing the trigger of the double-action revolver. The third shot brought a howl of pain and then someone repeating endlessly, "Help me."

But Jessica wasn't going to step out there to try to help an unseen gunman.

"How many did you see?" she asked Reggie.

"Just the one, but there may have been another one nearer the horses."

"Two, anyway," Jessie said. "I caught the muzzle flash from two weapons."

They waited in the darkness, watching as night crept in. Jessica was shivering. Reggie was beside her, and in his hand was a small silver-plated pistol she hadn't known he was carrying.

She frowned, still wondering about the man yet knowing that he had saved her life by throwing her to the ground at the instant the gunman rose from cover.

"Help me."

He was still out there, moaning. But no one could help him now. He had chosen to gamble and he'd lost. He was paying the price—painful death in the cold of the wilderness.

After another ten minutes Jessica heard a horse being ridden away. The other outlaw had made his escape. She let more long minutes pass before finally she nodded at Reggie and they rose to walk to where the sniper lay.

"Dead," Reggie said.

He was all of that. Dark, twisted, his face still showing the pain of death. Jessie didn't have a lot of sympathy for him. He had come looking to kill and he had paid the price.

She had nerve but she didn't much like dipping into his pockets. One of them was filled with blood. Still, it was in that one that she found a coin. She drew it out, wiping it on the dead man's filthy coat.

"What's that?" Reggie asked.

It shone in the light of the coming moon. Dully, softly shone. What it was was a Prussian gold coin.

"Where would the man come by a Prussian coin?" Reggie asked.

"I don't know," Jessie answered, although she did know

70

very well. The cartel paid in cash. She put the coin in the pocket of her vest, not saying anything more. But it stuck in her mind—Reggie knew instantly what sort of coin that was. He knew, but he hadn't seemed surprised.

What did that mean, if anything? She didn't know.

One thing Jessica Starbuck did know: The night had lost its charm and there wasn't any magic at all left in returning to a castle with this dark and mysterious knight. There was only uneasiness.

"Let's go," Jessica said abruptly. She needed suddenly to see Ki, to discuss this with someone she knew she could trust.

Ki wasn't there, however. At that moment he was talking to the Utes on the White River. From the castle walls he had seen a fire and now, after a hard ride, he was standing looking at the destruction the fire had caused.

"All my corn," Chi-Tha said morosely. "All of Miwok's corn. All of Huapa's corn..." he went on as if it were a chant learned long ago, a prayer, his voice a monotone. "All of Ka-lipa's corn."

"How did it start?" Ki asked.

"The ghost came," the Indian said. "Spanish ghost came and his eyes started these fires."

Ki didn't argue with the Ute. If the old man believed it, he wasn't going to talk him out of it. "There was just the one man?" Ki asked, crouching down to let his fingers rake through the still warm ashes. Acre after acre had been destroyed by the blaze. There wasn't much left for the Utes to count on for winter provisions.

"One man," Chi-Tha said distractedly. "It was a mistake to settle here. We are hunters, nomads. We should have wandered the world."

"This is a good place to live," Ki said and the old Indian

71

looked at him as if surprised to find him still there. "There is water and grass, and the soil is fertile."

"It is not good land! It is haunted."

"Not haunted," Ki said.

"Haunted, yes." Chi-Tha had made his mind up and that was that.

"So what will you do?"

The Indian looked at the tall man, the man with the quiet eyes, the man who moved like a panther. The man who Chi-Tha knew was a warrior.

"We will move." He shrugged. "What is there to do? We shall go back into the hills and we will hunt. The life will be harder, but we shall not have the spirit of the dead to contend with."

"Don't move, Chi-Tha," Ki said, "not yet. Give me time to help you."

"To help us? By driving the spirit away?"

"Yes," Ki said, "just that. If you leave now, Chi-Tha, life will be much harder for your young for years to come. If you leave, others will move on to this land, others who covet it."

"The white ranchers?"

"No." Ki stood and looked up into the mountains, toward the distant castle. "Not the ranchers. There are other men who want this land. It would take too long to explain, Chi-Tha, but I want you to trust me for just a little while more. I do not want you to leave this land."

"Why should I trust you? You are a man from across the sea. What do you know about the necessary magic, about the Spanish curse? The shaman has chanted and made smoke and fasted. What more can you do, Ki? How can you help the people of Chi-Tha?"

"Perhaps I can't," Ki said, "but I will try. I will find the spirit of the Spanish man and I shall drive him from your land."

"Before many are killed? Before many are hungry, Ki?" the Ute asked.

"Before then. I vow it," Ki said, "and my vow means much."

The Ute watched Ki's eyes for a long while before he finally nodded agreement. "All right. I will keep the people here—for now. But if there is blood, Ki, if a Ute dies, it will now be on your head."

There wasn't any response to make to that, so Ki only nodded once, watching as the old man drew his blanket more tightly around his shoulders against the coolness of evening and walked off through the ash toward the Ute village beyond.

"It is," Ki said under his breath, "now on my head."

It was getting late now. Darkness was settling in and the Utes were going home to eat, to sit by the cooking fires quietly and tell tales of Spanish ghosts, to fill their bellies with corn soup and venison, and to lie down with their women.

Ki watched the fires silently for a long while. Not the fires of the Ute camp, but the other, distant fires, which he had first taken for the bonfire from Camden. A low reddish glow stained the dark hills to the west, higher up toward the Rockies.

It was too far south to be from Camden, too far west and south to be the castle. And just who else, Ki wondered, could it be. The country around here was empty, nearly unpopulated. The fire, however, was large or else there were many of them. Many fires for many men.

Whose men?

Ki recovered his sorrel horse and swung aboard, riding

out of the Indian camp. By then the fires in the hills had gone out, but Ki had marked their location. He would find them, and whatever secrets the hills held, Ki vowed he would discover them.

"The cartel," he told the uncaring horse, "does not plan a job of this size and merely send out one man costumed as a knight."

There would have to be other people to move in if the Utes proved recalcitrant. There would have to be a leader, perhaps a high-ranking cartel man, perhaps one high enough to be able to give Jessie and Ki the name they wanted more than any other—the name of the man who had ordered the death of Alex Starbuck and his wife.

Ki rode higher into the cold, dark hills, the moon at his back. Once, distantly, he thought he heard several gunshots, but he couldn't be sure.

He became lost several times. It wasn't a simple task riding the unfamiliar hills in darkness. The rising moon helped some, but even with its silver illumination, Ki wandered aimlessly for a long while, once finding himself on a precipice which overhung the basin below and from which there was no trail leading downward.

The fires had been put out, but their scent lingered in the air and by that scent Ki finally found what he was looking for.

Deep in the pines above the basin he found his objective—the camp that lay still and dark but not entirely asleep on the mountain slope.

He spotted the camp as he crested the wooded rise, and well aware of the moonlight that shone brightly down across the land, Ki instantly swung his sorrel aside, riding back into the trees.

He tied the horse loosely and slipped silently back toward the forest.

He could see the smallest pinpoints of light below, the still glowing embers of dead fires, and he could estimate the number of men there by the moonlight.

They had plenty of help. Thirty to forty was Ki's guess. Men who would be used as a last resort, to ride through the White River Basin killing every man, woman, and child, white or Indian, if it became necessary for the cartel to abandon stealth and go to brute force for its planned take-over.

Ki glanced at the moon, at the ridge behind the camp. Then he made his decision to go in. He had to know for sure.

"It is you," he whispered to the night. "Deadly and dark, it is the cartel."

Still he had to be sure. His mind needed evidence to back the feeling that was in his bones. He started down.

Ki was swift and silent. Darkness covered his movements. Now and then he heard a horse, now and then a muttering voice.

He was working his way down a slope rife with flowering purple sage and chia when a guard unexpectedly rose from the underbrush.

"Hey—" the man said, and his shotgun started to come up toward Ki's body.

He didn't have the chance to say anymore, to do anymore. Ki half turned away and kicked out, his foot slamming the gun from the guard's hands. The samurai never stopped. He bored in, whirling and twisting, and as the confused cartel thug tried to back away, Ki backheeled him and he went down hard. When the man tried to rise to a sitting position, Ki administered a middle-knuckle punch, a *nakadata,* to the center of the man's forehead, and he sagged back, instantly unconscious.

Ki winged the shotgun away, looked around from his

crouched position, and started on again.

He could see sleeping men, their horses bunched in a box canyon beyond the camp, and now as he neared the camp he could hear voices again and understand the words that drifted to his ears.

"Damned Starbuck brat..."

"Don't worry about...she'll live to regret all of her damned tricks."

There were four of them, sitting around a tiny fire outside an army tent. From time to time a bottle was passed from one man to another. Ki looked closely but he could recognize none of the men. He lay there in the sage-scented darkness knowing that he was playing with fire. If they found him, they would do their best to finish him.

The men had decided that drinking was more important than conversation and they fell into silence, sipping whiskey, growing drunk slowly, watching the fire burn out. There was nothing more to be learned apparently, so Ki started away, crawling backward into the brush, then following a dark gully toward the crest where he had left his horse.

The trouble was others had found his horse.

Ki jogged through the trees and into the clearing where the sorrel stood. The first man had a Winchester and he was grinning as he jabbed the muzzle of it at Ki, shouting, "This is it, my friend."

That was it but it didn't happen the way the man thought. Ki saw the man with the rifle and the other one standing beside the sorrel, pistol drawn. Both of them were far too confident.

Ki didn't try to swerve away. He kept on running, diving into a long roll that brought him up under the muzzle of the Winchester as the gun discharged, splitting the night with flame and sound, kicking up a fountain of dust and pine needles as the bullet went across Ki's shoulder and hit the ground beneath the trees.

Ki, who had never stopped rolling, came up with his shoulder beneath the cartel man's chin. The impact snapped the man's head back and Ki heard teeth breaking, felt hot blood spray him.

The one with the pistol tried a shot, but it wasn't all that easy in the darkness and he missed. He only got one try.

Ki came to his feet with a razor-edged *shuriken* in his hand. He flicked it toward the gunman whose face registered momentary disbelief. He had seen nothing in the Japanese man's hand, had seen nothing of the missile flying toward him. He had only felt a sudden hard thump against the middle of his forehead, a shot like a mule's kick, and then the blood which began to flow down his face.

He had felt that and then nothing more as his brain, sharpened steel imbedded in it, gave up trying to sort out the confused images and sank into the cold oblivion of the long night.

Ki looked the bodies over, recovered his *shuriken*, and with a last glance at the camp below him, swung aboard the sorrel.

The shots would have been heard, so there was no time to delay. He heeled the horse and headed down the slope into the deeper shadows of the forest.

The castle by moonlight was eerie. Men moved along the battlements like ancient guards. They were only workmen still at their job. Ki came out of the darkness and into the firelit courtyard and was scarcely noticed.

It was unreal with men moving this way and that, lugging wooden panels and timbers, stone and mortar, furnishings. Ki walked his horse for a few minutes, then led it to the cold stable where great chargers stood. Ki rubbed his own horse down and then looked around.

The horses were all dry, all wearing blankets. But one of them had been out that evening, one of them belonged to the man who had burned the Indians' corn.

After this length of time there wasn't any way to determine which horse it had been. Besides, Ki was beginning to wonder—despite Carrie's certainty—whether the black knight was actually riding out of the castle. It seemed more likely that he had another base. There were many eyes around the castle. With the work going on around the clock, an emerging dark knight would surely be noticed.

Ki was suddenly tired. He couldn't come up with any fresh ideas. Maybe Jessica had learned something worth knowing. In the morning they would compare notes. For now Ki just wanted to put his head down on a pillow.

He went out of the stable and started toward his chambers using the arched gallery to his left. Dark and still. No firelight reached Ki's eyes.

Yet he could hear, and well enough to become aware that there was someone following him.

So, I wasn't quick enough, he thought. Not quick enough off the mountain, away from the secret cartel camp in the hills. They had been summoned by the shots and had followed him—maybe.

He walked on, varying his pace. As he entered the long dining hall, he paused. The man behind him paused, too. Ki frowned and went on, climbing the stairway to the second story where his sleeping chamber was.

Below, he still heard the steps. Soft, scurrying, then growing cautious at the stairway.

"Come on," Ki murmured, "let us finish this charade."

From the way the stalker moved, Ki became convinced that the man knew the castle, knew it very well indeed. Perhaps he hadn't been followed so very far at all. Maybe it was Ethelbert back there—or Reggie. *Despite* Jessie's

78

feelings about the young peer, Ki didn't trust him. There was something about the man that Ki didn't like—or, as much as he hated to admit the presence of such feelings, maybe Ki was simply jealous.

"Come on," Ki whispered, but there now seemed to be no one below, no one he could see or hear. Was his own imagination working overtime, prodded by the strangeness of the surroundings, by this dark and dismal place, this place of haunts and spirits?

Ki shook off that mood and went to his room. Inside, he lit a candle and then after a reasonable length of time he blew it out.

But he didn't go to bed. He stood beside his door, waiting. Maybe imagination was at work, but Ki had been hunted many times, had thugs stalk him, some of them very good at their trade, and he thought he knew when he was being pursued.

A minute later a soft footstep caused him to smile slightly. The faintest scuff of leather against stone, a whisper was all that it was, but Ki had heard it and the sound was distinct—someone coming cautiously, too cautiously to be a friend.

The door opened a bare fraction of an inch and Ki tensed, his body like a spring, alert and ready, his eyes seeing better now, his ears sensitive as the darkness and the adrenaline combined to bring his survival instincts to full awareness.

The door opened another few inches and Ki went for the intruder's wrist. He yanked and simultaneously kicked the door shut, whirling the stalker into his room.

"Oh, Mr. Ki! It's only me, Carrie."

And it was Carrie, her woman's body soft and warm beneath Ki's warrior's hands.

"Whatever were you thinking, Mr. Ki?" she asked. She touched her breasts with her fingertips. Her dark hair was

79

down, her eyes wider than ever. She wore a sheer white nightgown, and whatever Ki *had* been thinking, he was thinking something else just then as he scooped her up and took her to his bed.

# Chapter 8

She was a laughing thing, soft and willing. She nearly tugged Ki from the bed as she pulled his trousers off.

"Now you owe me," Carrie said. "Now you do, Mr. Ki, for assaulting me like that."

The trousers flew from Ki's hips and Carrie staggered backward. She lifted her nightdress over her head and by starlight and moonlight Ki saw her sturdy, bouncy body as she crossed to him.

"Oh, my, Mr. Ki, now that is a nice one you've got there. I should like to just hold it for a time and then sit on it if I may. Oh, my!"

She followed through with her plan. With Ki on his back on the big bed, Carrie climbed up and squatted over him, holding his erection with both hands, tugging at it as she smiled at Ki. From time to time she touched the head of his shaft to her crotch, which was damp and warm and tantalizing. Ki let the palms of his hands roam her breasts, her firm thighs, her full, rounded buttocks.

"Now I don't want to tease you, Mr. Ki," Carrie said. "Now you tell me if it's too much for you, will you?"

It was getting to be. She was eager and ready and Ki said, "Put it in, will you?"

Carrie smiled again and did just that, slowly settling, taking Ki's length into her as she bent forward and kissed his lips lightly, her inner muscles working on Ki's shaft.

"Oh, my, Mr. Ki," she said, falling against him, her body warm and soft. Ki could feel the woman come undone inside, feel the spasmic movements of her body. "Oh, my, Mr. Ki!"

She worked against him diligently, reaching back to touch him, to cup his sac in her hand. "Please do it now, Mr. Ki," she breathed into his ear. "I want to feel it. Please."

And since Ki was a gentleman, he came as she held him, as she nibbled at his ear, her breath warm and moist against his throat.

They lay together, their bodies cooling, and the night was silent except for Carrie's occasional contented sigh.

It was long after midnight when Ki awoke. Carrie was gone. It was damned cool without her and he reached for his shirt, trying to remember what had awakened him.

And then he heard it again and he knew.

Ki leaped from the bed and looked upward at the narrow windows, windows designed for an archer and not to admit sunlight. He stepped on a bureau and chinned himself, peering out at the dark valley in time to see the dark knight disappearing into the forest beyond, the rattle of his armor faint and metallic.

Ki was in his trousers and slippers in minutes. He stepped into the corridor to find it dark and cold. Jessica was there peering from her doorway.

82

"What is it?" she asked. She was sleep-tousled, her hair in an appealing tangle.

"I just saw the knight leave. I'm going to follow him," Ki said.

"Wait for me."

"No, not this time. I don't want to wait, number one— and number two, I'd like you to do something that may be more productive."

"Yes?" Jessica Starbuck was smiling faintly. In his excitement Ki had gotten a little bossy. He didn't notice her slight mockery.

"There's a man missing from Castle Whitechapel right now. Sir John, Ethelbert, or Reginald—maybe someone else, I don't know, but whoever he is, he's the dark knight. If I can't catch him tonight, maybe we'll still be able to find out who it is."

"We could both do that, Ki. Search the castle to see who's missing."

"We could," Ki said a little grimly, "but I made a promise to an old man, to a people. I told them that I would banish this spirit who was bothering them. I can't let the knight do more damage, if that's what he has in mind."

"All right," Jessie agreed. It wasn't time for debate. If Ki had any hope of catching the knight, he was going to have to go now. "Get going. I'll poke around here."

"But with care."

"Sure." Jessica smiled. "With care."

He hesitated, but then realizing he had to move quickly, he turned and started down the corridor at a trot, his cork-soled slippers silent and swift.

He went down the stairs at a dangerous clip, taking them three and four at a time until he bounded to the floor of the dining hall and out along the arched corridor to the stables.

If a horse was missing, Ki didn't see which one it was, nor did he know who owned which animal. There would be time to consider all of that later. For now, there was hardly time to throw a saddle on the back of the sorrel and bridle it.

Ki swung aboard and urged the horse out through the strangely empty courtyard. Where were the workers? Given the night off?—it was possible. It was Saturday night.

He was across the drawbridge and out on the grassy valley in minutes, leaning low across the withers of the horse, pursuing a black knight through the wilderness forest.

Meanwhile, Jessica had dressed, and after strapping on her Colt revolver, she stepped into the silent corridor. There was a breeze twisting through the castle from no apparent source. Maybe the currents were due to the architect's design; maybe these moving breezes had given rise to stories about ghosts and spirits.

Maybe.

Jessica walked the long gallery, moving toward the room where Sir John Whitechapel slept—or was supposed to sleep.

She approached the room cautiously, keeping her eyes moving, glancing back across her shoulder. She, too, was now aware that the work around the castle had ceased, that it was an empty place, cold and stony.

She touched the butt of her pistol from time to time, taking comfort in knowing that there were five .38 loads at her command.

Nevertheless, Jessie was anxious. There's little pleasure to be derived from slipping around in your host's house in the dead of night. Especially when your host just may be a murderer and the house happens to be a castle with its own cold secrets.

She found Sir Whitechapel's room more by touch than

sight. The corridor was dark, empty, cold. A chill, which seemed to have an otherworldly origin, crept down Jessie's spine, probing at her.

Imagination, she told herself angrily. Once her father had told her, "It's a great gift but it can be a great foe, imagination."

She paused before Whitechapel's door and slowly wrapped hesitant fingers around the iron handle. Taking a slow breath, she opened the door. It squeaked faintly and Jessie's pulse lifted a little.

If Whitechapel had heard that, it would mean trouble. At the least he would be offended, outraged; at the most, he would decide that it was time to finish off this interloper.

There wasn't anything to worry about. Whitechapel wasn't in his bed.

Jessie stood in the doorway for a long minute, seeing the high, narrow windows—blue and dim—the empty bed, the barren, high-ceilinged room.

"It's him," she said to herself. "Whitechapel is behind all of this."

But why? He was hardly the typical cartel hireling. Unless he was himself a cartel officer. And why not? Hadn't he been involved in international trade before this so-called retirement? Hadn't he admitted that he knew Alex Starbuck? Knew him and killed him?

That started a long string of unhappy memories, which Jessie couldn't afford to indulge just then. She pushed the thoughts away and eased out of the room.

Reggie.

She needed to talk to Reggie. Reggie who had some burden he carried with him. The knowledge that his father was a criminal?

She started down the hall again, working her way toward Reggie's room. She smiled to herself as she thought of

85

various interesting ways of awakening the man.

She didn't have the chance to utilize any of those ideas—Reggie's bed was empty.

She stood staring at the empty bed and the blood began to thump in her temples. There could be a hundred reasons for his not being there in the middle of the night—she knew that, but didn't believe it.

Something sinister was happening here and it wasn't nearly over. There would be more blood, much blood, and Reginald Whitechapel was somehow involved.

Jessie backed from the room, silently closing the door. She had made it her business to find out where Ethelbert's room was, and now although it seemed perfunctory, she went there, too.

*Empty.*

And his bed hadn't been slept in. The entire family was out. Somewhere. Doing something. Jessica silently cursed. She hadn't proven a thing—except that something was up.

Maybe, however, she had proven that there was no significance in Reggie's not being in his room. No one was in tonight, it seemed. A dinner in town? A project she knew nothing about that had kept the family out late? It seemed possible ... except that someone had gone out of the castle on this night, dressed in a suit of armor, intent on doing harm, and Ki was out following him.

"Don't let it be Reggie," she said, but she was too much the realist not to understand that it could very well be Reggie. Reggie, the champion of Castle Whitechapel, Reggie who painted a self-portrait of himself as a dark knight.

She heard it then—a whispering, a murmuring from the depths of the castle. A conversation secretive and angry. Jessica cocked her head and listened.

Nothing.

It might have been her imagination, she thought, but it

wasn't, for as she walked another few steps down the corridor, she heard it again. Voices in the bowels of the castle. Reggie and his father, his uncle? Or was it a cartel meeting, the coven of killers?

She had to know. Her throat was constricted and her blood humming in her ears. The pistol had found its way into her hand as she crept down the stairs to the main floor, the distant voices growing louder.

But where were they?

She was in the dining hall, which had begun to resemble its completed form, flags hanging on the walls, the table set with silverplate, the Turkish carpets on the floor, the tapestries in place.

Jessica moved slowly across the room, listening. There was no doorway, no flight of stairs, where her ears led her. And then there was.

She halted next to a paneled wall, tilted her head, and leaned a hand against the wall. And the panel in the wall slid open.

Jessica jumped back. She stood indecisively for a minute, hearing the voices, louder now but no clearer, seeing a faint light below.

They didn't go down there to get up a poker game, she thought and she started on, not liking it much, knowing she had to do it. She needed to know what was going on here and who was behind it. With any luck she would surprise the principals as they sat making their plans.

She moved down the stone steps. She was barefoot and the stones were cold against her feet. Below the voices droned on. It didn't seem to be English. The cadences seemed wrong. There seemed to be a lot of gutturals. The staircase wound around a huge stone pillar. A torch had been set into an iron holder there.

Rats scuttled away—had they, too, been imported? There

87

was an unhealthy smell to the place. The moss had already resumed its growth. The castle might have been dismantled and rebuilt, but it was still hundreds of years old and it smelled of decay, of death.

What had the original owner of this castle used the dungeon for?

Jessica reached a landing, twenty by twelve feet long. Two doorless passageways opened off it. The sounds of voices continued to rise.

And then they stopped.

Jessie's heart began to race and the hand clenching her revolver became cramped. She was holding it that tightly. Had they heard her? Seen her?

The torch behind her flickered out and Jessica spun that way, her pistol coming up. There was no one there, nothing but the darkness. And that was all there was below. The light in the lower chamber had gone out as well, and now Jessica was stranded there on the landing in utter blackness.

She hesitated again. They would expect her to turn, to flee, to work her way back up the stairs as rapidly as possible. And someone just might be waiting for her up there. One shove and she would topple from the steps to the stone floor below.

Besides, she wouldn't have a chance of solving this thing if she retreated now. She had a revolver and she knew how to use it. She had Starbuck courage.

"You can't hide from me," she whispered to the darkness, "like a bunch of damned rats."

She started down, feeling her way.

As she eased down the steps, her left hand was on the wall; her right held the Colt .38. She moved slowly, a step or two at a time, pausing to listen, to stare into the darkness.

They didn't give themselves away. If they were down there, they were silent and very patient. Maybe they weren't down there at all. Maybe there was another way out of the dungeon.

From far above, the heavy sound of footsteps rang. Jessie looked that way. There was no light but someone was coming, someone who knew the way well enough to travel it in darkness.

She wanted to get off the stairs and on to level ground. Forgetting caution, she started on, hurrying now. Her foot went from under her as she missed a step, and Jessica toppled forward, falling ten feet or more before she landed flat on her bottom on the dungeon's stone floor.

She moved hurriedly, silently, to one side.

The footsteps had stopped. There was no sound at all but the thump of her heart, of her breath that seemed to squeak in and out of her lungs.

It was right in front of her suddenly, lunging from the darkness. It—or he. A thing with a sword raised and Jessie fired three times, moving to one side as the broadsword struck down and rang off the stone wall behind her.

The Colt blazed away, its report echoing angrily through the dungeon of Whitechapel Castle. The flame from the muzzle illuminated the scene briefly, but it was a confusion of images that Jessie's mind couldn't assimilate properly—then or later.

A man in a mailed shirt with a broadsword trying to decapitate her. Behind him a row of dark creatures, men or spirits, a table with papers on it, a map on the far wall, some ancient instrument of torture with great wooden wheels. The flame spewing from the muzzle of the Colt illuminated that all in one brief fraction of a second, and then the darkness settled again like heavy liquid.

There were men moving away from her, cautious feet, and she called out, "Stand where you are!" but they kept moving and she had to let them go. She couldn't stand there emptying her gun into the darkness.

The swordsman at her feet groaned horribly. Then the death rattle sounded in his throat and he was still and quiet.

Jessie was alone again, alone in the darkness. There was still someone above her, on the stairs. She didn't want to go that way, but she wasn't crazy about going on ahead. She decided to do it anyway—those men had known another way out, and they hadn't been armed or expected Jessica to be. A small miscalculation had cost them.

She eased her way forward, toward the corridor the escaping cartel men had used. It was black as Hades at first, but after thirty slow steps there seemed to be light entering the dungeon from somewhere.

It took Jessie a hell of a long time to find it, but finally she located it. An ill-fitting oaken door set into the wall. It took only a little pressure to open it and pass through to the other staircase beyond. At the head of this, she found open air, lantern light, and a moon beaming down out of a clear sky.

She walked away from the entranceway, which was beneath the outer wall. She put a half mile between herself and the castle and then, in the dark, tall pines, she sat down, holstered her pistol, and slowly breathed the cool, open air. Behind her the castle stood dark and menacing, and just for a moment Jessica Starbuck had a thought that gave her deep pleasure to nourish.

"A bundle of dynamite. Not much—twelve sticks in the dungeon. A three minute fuse and the whole thing would be over, and good riddance."

But the mood passed, the moment of frustration. She knew she should return to the dungeon, try to identify the dead man, see what the papers she had noticed on the table might be, but she didn't have the nerve to do it. Not on that night, not then. Maybe when Ki returned.

90

And where was Ki? Ki who had gone riding after the dark knight. Ki who was alone out there with what could only be described as a madman.

"Be careful, Ki," Jessie said to the darkness. "You just be careful. Whatever this is we've stumbled on, it's deadly, very deadly."

# Chapter 9

Ki sat on the sorrel horse as it drank from the White River. The moon was bright on the dark water, streaking it with gold. The Ute camp was quiet and Ki was puzzled.

"Where is he? He should have been here by now."

Unless, of course, the dark knight had gone to the hidden cartel camp for some reason, some sort of conference with the bosses ... or, and Ki's stomach knotted, unless he had gone to one of the ranches upriver.

It had seemed logical in Ki's mind that the knight would attack the Utes again. They, after all, were the ones who had nurtured the superstition of the Spanish curse; they were the ones who feared the iron suit. The Hicks family obviously didn't fear him. Mrs. Hicks had used that iron suit as a target for her rifle.

Therefore, it had to have been the Utes the black knight came after ... had to be, but it wasn't. Ki knew that with sudden certainty.

"The bastard's gone after one of the white ranchers this time."

But which one and how could Ki hope to cut him off on the sorrel that had been ridden through most of the day and a good part of the night?

"Come on," Ki said, pulling the balky sorrel's muzzle from the water with a sharp tug on the reins. It would do no good to have the horse's belly full of cold water. There was some long riding to do.

Ki turned the horse northward, and as the moon started its descent toward the Rockies, he urged the little sorrel toward the three ranches.

Everything seemed quiet at the J-Bar, the Jankowitz place, when Ki reached it a grueling hour later. The house was dark, the chimney cold. Recalling Jankowitz's belligerence, Ki was careful about approaching the house directly.

Instead, he circled the building, moving on horseback through the oak trees. The lowering moon followed him, painting crooked shadows beneath his horse.

He could see nothing at all out of order and he swore silently.

Wrong again? he thought. What if the knight had indeed planned on hitting the Ute village but had stopped, for some reason, at the cartel camp?

There was no point in worrying if he was wrong or not. Ki had settled on his plan of action; there was nothing to do but carry it through.

The Jankowitz place was apparently unmolested, so Ki rode toward his next stop, the Wertz ranch. The sorrel was leg weary, running with its head low so that eventually Ki was forced to slow up, to walk it northward as the night passed.

He walked on, the night growing colder. The river was a cold silver ribbon beside his trail.

Shots cut the night's silence with violent repetitiveness. Ki's head came up. He slapped the sorrel with his knees and drove it forward through the willow brush and cotton-woods toward the Wertz ranch, where the gunfire had increased to a savage crescendo.

He could see stabbing flame now and he slowed the horse, circling wide. It wouldn't do anybody much good for him to ride into a crossfire.

Ki stopped the sorrel and swung down before it had staggered to a complete halt. Circling through the oaks, he filled his hand with a *shuriken*. His eyes continued to move as he ran, to measure the forces of battle.

From two windows of the house, gunfire spat defiance at the night—that would be Wertz and his son. From the trees ahead of Ki, four or five rifles answered the fire.

He grew tired of doing it on his own, Ki thought. The black knight had brought help with him this time, modern weapons in the hands of cartel men. The guns continued to blast away as Ki came across the first cartel thug.

At Ki's footfall the man turned, bringing the muzzle of his long-barreled Henry repeater up. Ki flipped his *shuriken* underhanded at the rifleman and it caught throat muscle, arteries, and trachea, instantly killing the cartel hireling.

Ki leaped over the body and ran through the oak grove, working his way toward a gun that was being fired methodically from behind a clump of boulders to his right.

This one went silently, nearly painlessly. Ki was behind him before the man heard him or saw him. Like a death wind, Ki slipped through the trees to his man. His forearm looped around the sniper's throat, and his hand twisted his skull forward. With a snap of bone, nerves were severed in the thug's neck and he died without making a sound. Ki let him sag to the earth; then he picked up the man's hat and slipped into his jacket, which stunk of sweat.

Ki started on, still jogging.

The third man was beyond the trees, beside the new barn. Rifle fire from the house peppered the green wood and the cartel man, cursing, reloaded. Looking up, he saw Ki rushing toward him.

"Damn all, Ed, you'll scare a man to death," he growled.

Then Ki scared him to death.

Forked, stiff fingers jabbed at the cartel man's eyes, and a chopping hand slashed downward, striking the base of his neck. The double blow was quite efficient, quite deadly.

From the corner of his eyes, Ki saw the man he wanted. Sitting on a huge charger, the black knight watched. Then, as Ki rose to pursue him, he stuck the big horse with his spurs and it leaped into clanking motion. Ki jumped in pursuit.

But he didn't get far. From the house the Wertzes, father and son, peppered the corner of the barn with .44s and Ki had to throw himself back to shelter as the knight's horse reached its stride and galloped away.

Ki threw aside his borrowed hat and coat and tentatively stuck his head out from behind the barn. "Wertz!" he called.

"Yeah?" the suspicious voice answered. "Who the hell's that?"

"Ki. You met me a few days ago. The Japanese man."

"Yeah, are you in this after all?"

"In this, yes—but on your side. Listen, Wertz, it's over out here. They're all down or run off. I'm going after the leader." There was no answer for a long while. "Do you hear me?"

"I hear you—why should I believe you?" Wertz demanded.

"Just do it," Ki said, losing patience. The knight was getting farther away. "Don't shoot. I'm going after the man in armor. Please, Wertz!"

Again there was no answer. Finally it came.

It was young Wertz, panic-stricken, who said, "Ki! I need you here. Pa's bleeding something awful."

"All right. Hold your fire."

Ki looked across his shoulder in the direction the dark knight had gone; then, grinding his teeth he started toward the house.

There wasn't much to be done for Wertz. By the time Ki entered the house and found the boy crouched over his father, the ricochet he had taken had done its work.

The younger Wertz's face was anguished, white as ivory. He looked to Ki for help but there was nothing Ki could do. The blood had drained out of the man; neither of them could pour it back in.

Wertz had time to say one thing to each of them before he died. He took his son's hand and said, "Stand tall, boy."

To Ki he simply said, "Get 'em."

Ki closed his eyes then and stood. The boy looked to Ki for something Ki couldn't give him—solace, endurance. "What can we do?" Wertz asked.

"Just what he told us," Ki answered. "Stand tall."

"I'll stand tall, by God," Wertz said, blood rushing back into his face. "I'll follow that son of a bitch and kill him!"

"No." Ki placed a hand on the boy's forearm, restraining him. "We will do what we were told—*I* was told to get them, remember?"

"But—"

"You do what must be done here. If you are killed, the ranch will be lost. There is nothing your father would have desired less. You remain—sometimes that's harder than rushing off with a gun; I know it. But believe me, I am better equipped to find this man, to kill him, than you are."

The anger, the frustration, slowly drained out of Wertz. He wasn't a fighter by nature. He was a rancher, that was

97

all. He would do what he had been told.

"Can you help me . . . carry him outside. I'd like to bury him near where we put my mother down."

They did that and then Ki left the man to his unhappy duty. He found the sorrel, which had stiffened up and wasn't in any mood to travel, and swung aboard. Then he began to ride toward the castle beyond the hills, the castle where the solution to this was, where a man who did murder in the dead of night lived.

The moon went orange and sank behind the peaks of the high mountains and the land went dark, but Ki knew the way now. He found the castle dark, nearly asleep. What had Jessie found out this night? Would she know which of the Whitechapel men had been out?

"I hope so," Ki said under his breath, "I sincerely hope so." That had been no idle promise he made to Wertz. He would find the killer and the rancher would be avenged.

A sudden inexplicable splash of light beside the southern wall of the castle drew Ki's eye. He was still a mile off, but even from that distance he could tell that there was no work going on in that area, and unless his memory was unreliable, something it usually wasn't, there was no entrance there, either.

It intrigued Ki and despite his eagerness to meet with Jessica, he swung that way, riding down the black grassy slope toward the castle.

The moat stopped him. Dark and deep and remotely sinister, it blocked his way. Ki frowned and, after a minute, swung down. It was only a puzzle briefly. Then he found the planks hidden in the bushes and he placed them across the moat.

Looking around and then up toward the parapet high above, he crossed over, leaving the sorrel.

He found nothing but a blank stone wall—at first.

His searching hands found the iron hinges and, seconds later, the latch that opened a concealed door.

It was a silent thing, this ancient door. The hinges had been oiled recently. The door was just tall enough for a horse to enter, and as the door opened Ki smelled horse.

He slipped into the corridor beyond the door and closed the entrance behind him. Walking down a long earthen ramp, he found himself suddenly in a stable, having entered by an unseen passage.

He hadn't learned much, but he had discovered how the black knight left the castle without being seen.

Were all these old places filled with secret passageways and hidden rooms? Probably. In times of trouble a beleaguered nobleman needed a way to make a hasty, unseen exit.

Ki let those thoughts flit briefly through his mind; then he turned to something more practical. He had been on the heels of the black knight this time. The sorrel, weary as it had been, had closed ground on the armored charger of the knight. Somewhere in that stable was a horse that would show signs of being ridden hard and long that night. There hadn't been time for the knight to cool it and rub it, time for the horse's body to settle back into its normal, resting rhythms.

Ki moved along from stall to stall, his hand resting on the flanks of the great horses. Until he felt the heat rising from one of them, felt the sweat on the horse's hide.

"Looking for something?"

At the sound of the voice, Ki spun and began to crouch. All that produced was amusement on the face of Reginald Whitechapel.

"It's very late," Whitechapel said.

Ki moved nearer the tall young man. "Late for both of us, Reginald."

99

"Yes." He made a casual, dismissive gesture. "There's much to do around here just now—for the family."

"I can imagine," Ki said, his eyes narrowed. He watched Reggie closely, trying to read his expression, trying to measure his man. He gave nothing away. He wasn't in armor, but that meant nothing. Maybe he had changed first and then come back to see to his horse.

"This is your animal, isn't it?" Ki asked.

Reggie smiled very thinly. "Yes. I wonder who was riding it tonight."

"Not you?"

"And if it was?" Reggie asked, his eyes meeting Ki's, briefly dueling with them.

"Then I would think that you might have been involved in a crime."

"A crime?"

"The crime of murder," Ki said.

Reggie shrugged, leaning against the stable partition. "I am no murderer. Are you some sort of investigator? A marshal or constable or whatever they have out here?"

"No. I am a man who has made a promise, a promise to avenge the murder."

"So?" Reggie nodded, rubbing his jaw with the back of his hand. "Then you are a dangerous man, are you not, Ki?"

"Perhaps. Are you?"

Reggie laughed out loud, but he said quite soberly, "Perhaps. Perhaps one day you shall discover if I am or not." Then he got a blanket from a trunk and began rubbing down the horse. Ki could tell he wasn't going to get anything more out of the champion of Whitechapel Castle and so after another minute he left.

By the time Ki had recovered his own horse, Reggie was gone from the stable. By the time Ki had grained the sorrel

100

and rubbed it down, it was nearly dawn and he walked up the gray, cold corridors to Jessie's room wearily.

When she answered the door, she looked somehow fresh, somehow beautiful if tousled. Exhaustion, worry, hard country living seemed unable to rob her of her freshness, her vitality.

"Ki! What happened?"

"It is," he said, "a very long story."

"Then sit down and let's hear it. When you're through, I've got a thing or two you might want to know."

Finished with his tale, Ki sat on the chair while Jessie, barefoot, elfin, perched on the bed. She told him everything that had happened that evening, about the visit to the dungeon and the attempt on her life.

When she was through, Ki shook his head heavily. "This is growing far too risky, Jessica."

"It's been risky since the day we decided to come after the cartel, Ki."

That was true. There wasn't much Ki could say in response. "You say that all three of them were absent from their beds—Reggie, his father, and Uncle Ethelbert?"

"That's correct, Ki."

"And where were they? At the meeting in the dungeon? Simply overseeing the work that was going on around the castle? I thought it would be a simple matter to determine who was missing tonight."

"I thought you'd decided that it was Reggie," Jessica commented. She was smiling slightly, but Ki found nothing funny in it.

"I don't know now," he had to admit. "The man has some arrogance about him, but is he a killer? All the same I wish you wouldn't have gone riding off alone with him."

"It was necessary," Jessie said, "a part of the investigation."

Ki shot her a flat glance. "I like this less and less," Ki said rising. "They can have no doubt that we are on to them now, none at all. Please, Jessica, keep your door locked and carry that revolver with you. I'm not overly fond of firearms, but it's obvious that the pistol is all that saved you tonight."

"From a fate worse than death?" she quipped.

"No," Ki said slowly, "only from death."

# Chapter 10

In the morning the combatants began to arrive. Knights from all corners of the world. Four of them had been on the same train out of Denver and had traveled together. Waldo, as he called himself, claimed to be Rumanian. Seth of Burgundy was French; Sir Peter Saxon and Lord George Austin represented Great Britain.

Whitechapel and his brother and son, dressed in their finery, greeted their guests and their valets, squires, and servants and escorted them to their rooms in the nearly completed castle. Everyone was introduced to Ki, whom they ignored for the most part after finding out he was not a member of their odd fraternity, and to Jessica, who wasn't ignored by any man anywhere.

Outside the walls, tents had started to go up; brightly striped, fringed, they should have been inhabited by medieval men and women, peddlers, craftsmen, smiths, tanners, bakers, and musicians with flutes and lyres. Instead

local retailers with their goods flocked to the grounds, sensing a big profit.

"No one will go thirsty," Ki observed as he and Jessica
toured the grassy area outside the castle where the fair was
being raised.

They had whiskey by the barrel, beer by the keg. It
seemed to be the main commodity. Wagonloads of the stuff
were rolled to the largest tents, which were in effect portable
saloons.

"There'll be people from all over the county up here,"
Jessica guessed. "A free show and plenty of liquor will
bring them pouring in."

"It will be easy for strangers to move around then," Ki
pointed out. Jessie barely heard him. She had just spotted
certain strangers who weren't taking any pains at all to
conceal themselves as they rode across the valley toward
Whitechapel Castle.

Seven men riding black horses and wearing dark suits
with narrow-brimmed hats were arriving. Behind them, other
men, lackeys or squires perhaps, led huge black chargers.
Other animals carrying packs followed them. There didn't
seem to be a spot of white, nor any other color but black,
in the entire outfit.

Jessie and Ki waited beside the trail as they came in,
men with dark eyes and thick eyebrows. They all could have
been cut from the same mold.

"Now what in blazes is this?" Jessie mused.

"Friendly, aren't they?"

"Are they alive?" Jessica asked.

"I think we should go back to the castle," Ki suggested.

Jessica nodded. She had the same idea Ki had. Maybe
they *weren't* cartel men, but if anyone had the right to be,
it was these seven black horsemen. They wanted to have a
closer look at things.

It wasn't hard to find them. Whitechapel had assembled all of his guests, old and new, in the great hall for wine and conversation. The dark men, still dusty, stood together with glasses in their hands, not drinking and hardly speaking.

Whitechapel saw Jessica. "Ah, Miss Starbuck, do come in."

Heads turned at the mention of her name. Dark eyes shifted toward her. Jessica crossed the room to where Whitechapel stood beside Ethelbert, who was glowering.

"You've met some of my friends, but not these gentlemen," Whitechapel said. "These are members of the Teutonic Knights, a very old fraternal organization. I'm sorry I don't know all of your names—this is Baron Von Rundstedt, their organizer and secretary."

One of the tall dark men bowed to Jessica. He reached for her hand but she couldn't bring herself to let him kiss it. He straightened up again, his eyes opaque, expressionless. Whitechapel waited, perhaps expecting Von Rundstedt to introduce the other members of the Teutonic Knights to Jessica, but he didn't seem interested in doing that.

"Our last member, Mr. Sato, arrived very early this morning," Whitechapel said. He turned slightly and nodded and it was only then that Jessica saw the Japanese in the corner. He was short, broad, and apparently muscular. His hair was tied like a samurai's and he wore a red sash around the waist of his dark western-style suit. He was staring not at Jessica but at Ki. After a minute the two men bowed curtly, and Whitechapel got on with his business.

"We are going to have the first draw if Reginald arrives . . . there he is, the prodigal," Whitechapel said and Reggie strode across the floor toward them. He stood possessively beside Jessica Starbuck, who tingled with his nearness despite her uncertainty about Reggie's motives.

"Where have you been?" he whispered.

"Walking."

"Walk with me next time."

His hand clasped hers and squeezed it quickly. It seemed to Jessie that everyone in the room saw it. Ethelbert was glowering at them, as was Von Rundstedt. Sato watched them, eyebrows arched.

"Now then, I have placed the name of each champion in this silver cup. I have included the names of my stepbrother, Ethelbert, and his squire who wishes to attempt to join our ranks. Joseph, where are you? Yes, this is Joseph Cavanaugh," Sir John said, introducing a sturdy but shy blond young man. "My brother's squire."

Whitechapel offered the silver bowl he held to Jessica, but she refused it. She wasn't going to have any part of this.

"Then I'll draw myself, if there are no objections." Whitechapel, smiling, tugged his sleeve up and drew the name of Von Rundstedt. "And his first opponent will be . . . Joseph Cavanaugh." Even Whitechapel didn't like that pairing. Cavanaugh seemed a little pale. Von Rundstedt showed as much expression as a block of stone. "Perhaps," Sir John said, "we should draw again."

"It's all right, Sir John," Cavanaugh said.

"For Christ's sake," Ethelbert said in annoyance, "that's the luck of the draw. Let's get on with it. What's the difference?"

Ethelbert's compassion was well hidden. Whitechapel, looking slightly worried and slightly annoyed, drew again, this time matching Sato with one of the Teutonic Knights. Reggie also drew one of the dark men. Ethelbert drew Waldo, the Rumanian. Seth of Burgundy drew Sir Peter, and Lord George Austin finished the pairings by drawing another of the Teutonic knights. The other dark knights would pair off against each other with one odd man sitting out the first round.

After the drawing was completed, there was more conversation and wine drinking. The conversation didn't interest Jessica and the wine drinking did nothing for Ki. They slipped out to stand in the courtyard where workmen were finishing the hanging of bunting from the walls of the castle.

"Well?" Ki asked.

"Cartel men."

Ki nodded. "Yes, I know they are—but there's no way to prove it. The question is what do they want here? I know that they want the White River Basin, but why all the rest of this foolishness?"

"I imagine they planned on using it as a cover. Who but you and I would know who they really are, what their real purpose is? If someone suspected troublemakers in the basin, it wouldn't be these highborn foreigners they considered."

"No, but . . ." Ki fell silent. Jessie turned toward him and saw his eyes on the doorway. There stood Reggie Whitechapel, tall, dark, serene. He strode toward Jessica.

"Hello, Ki. You don't mind if I take Jessie away for a while, do you? You two aren't getting the best hospitality we have to offer. Things will liven up, however."

"Will they?"

"Oh, I can promise that," Reggie said. He had stepped up beside Jessie and had taken her arm. "By the way, Ki, one of our guests seems to know you. He's talking about you in there. Very interesting."

"Is it?" Ki asked through tight lips.

"Yes, very interesting. You're something of a warrior yourself, aren't you?"

"I try not to fight for pleasure or for glory," Ki said.

107

"Unlike us?" Reggie laughed.

Jessie interrupted the tense dialogue. "Who was talking about Ki? One of the Teutonic Knights?"

"Why, no." Reggie's eyebrows drew together. "How would they know anything about our friend? It's his country-man who has been telling tales—Mr. Sato."

"You know him, Ki?" Jessie asked.

"I have . . . encountered him before. Mr. Sato is a latter-day samurai. A swaggering man. This sort of event must suit him perfectly. He has devoted a good part of his life to combat and subsequent bragging."

There was a bitterness there no one could fail to note. Jessie judged that this wasn't the time to delve into the relationship between Ki and Sato, however; with Reggie still an unknown quantity, Ki wouldn't want to open up.

He would be reluctant to open up, anyway, if it concerned his past. There wasn't much Jessie actually knew about Ki's background. He had told her some, but it was apparent that he held back much. His exit from Japan, she judged, had been bloody and hasty.

"Shall we go for a stroll," Reggie suggested. "Or a ride—would you like to ride out, Jessie?"

"Yes." She could read the meaning in his dark eyes and she nodded. She didn't trust this man fully, but her body needed him, her softer senses, her instincts trusted him next to her, wanted him on her, in her. "Let's ride out. Ki?"

"Yes, ride." He added, "But be careful."

Reggie Whitechapel laughed, "I'll be with her, Ki. What is there to worry about?"

Ki looked for a long while at the younger man, but instead of answering he touched Jessie's shoulder and walked away, back into the depths of the castle where the shouts of wine-enlivened knights echoed.

Reggie went to get the horses, returning with a bay horse

108

with a white stocking and the little dun Jessica had been riding.

"You all right?" Reggie asked.

"Yes, why?" She smiled brightly. Jessie swung aboard the dun, which shied a little, its hooves clacking on the stone courtyard.

Reggie rested his hand on her thigh as she sat looking down at him with her sea-green eyes. "You seem a little distracted," he told her.

"I was thinking."

"Yes?" He smiled and squeezed her leg.

"Not about that. Not entirely," she amended. Reggie took the bay's reins and swung up, and they started forward at a walk.

"About what?" he asked.

"This Joseph Cavanaugh. He seems a good boy."

"He is," Reggie agreed.

"And very young."

"Nearly eighteen. This is his first tournament, of course. He's been squiring for Ethelbert."

"What about this Von Rundstedt, Reggie? He seems very hard."

"He's hard. And very good, they say."

Jessie asked, "And brutal?"

It was a long time before Reggie answered. They walked their horses across the drawbridge and past the fair. "They say he is brutal," the man answered at last.

"Your father didn't seem pleased to have him paired against Von Rundstedt. Tell me, Reggie, there's no chance the boy will get hurt, is there?"

"Not badly hurt." Even that didn't seem to be the total truth. Reggie smiled quickly, faintly.

"How do they do it?" she asked. "How do they hold this combat?"

"Oh, well, they simply charge down the lists—two long enclosed runways—with padded lances, and if one man is knocked from his mount, he is eliminated."

"With padded lances?" Jessica asked.

"Oh, yes . . . the first rounds," he said in response.

"The first rounds," Jessie repeated. The sky was clear, the long grass waving in the wind. Beyond, the pines formed a dark green wall.

"Yes."

"But people have been hurt."

"Yes."

"Seriously."

Reggie shrugged. "I've seen it."

"And then after the first rounds. How is the final champion decided?" she demanded. "With padded lances and dull swords?"

He turned slowly toward her and he answered quite slowly. "The final champion," he told her, "is decided with pointed lances. With maces and sharpened swords. He is decided by a fight to the death."

Jessie looked at the man, expecting more, but there was no more. No more words, no more emotion. He didn't mention that if he were to win his early jousts it would be Reggie who was in a fight to death—perhaps against a friend, or his own uncle.

And if that happened, if Ethelbert killed Reggie, why, then, who would inherit Sir John's estates? Ethelbert, of course.

They entered the forest and the dark coolness seemed to shut out all those worries, just as they shut out the sunlight. They walked their horses up the winding trail, keeping close together, unspeaking.

They veered off the trail and into a deep cedar grove. Jessie looked around with surprise.

"This isn't the way to the cabin."

"No, I've found another rather private spot I want to show you."

"How private?"

"Private enough, I think," Reggie said and he reached over to slip his hand inside Jessie's blouse and cup the warm mound of her breast.

She looked at him, smiled, and slipped from her blouse. "Is that better?" she asked, although she hardly had to. There was a rapidly growing bulge at the crotch of his jeans as he let his eyes devour Jessica. Her round, firm breasts jiggled and bounced provocatively. Pale in the sunlight, pink-tipped, uptilted, they lifted Reggie's pulse to a hammering.

They climbed upward for another fifteen minutes until at last the trail terminated at a high ledge where grass and tiny silver-blue wildflowers grew in a fragrant carpet. The sun beamed brightly. Above them a pine clad bluff rose steeply, and below the long White River Basin stretched.

Reggie had thrown his own shirt aside as he dismounted, and now before Jessica's boot had touched ground he folded her into his arms, pressing his chest to her sun-warmed, soft breasts.

He kissed her deeply, then let his lips run down her neck to taste her nipples.

"Another hideaway?" Jessie asked, looking around the ledge.

"Another." Reggie was in no mood for conversation. He led Jessie to the edge of the grassy bluff and laid her down.

He knelt before Jessie and her fingers found his belt buckle, deftly undoing it before she worked down his trouser buttons, allowing him to spring free and draw her hands to him.

His shaft was alert and ready, teased by the ride up the mountain. Jessie rolled to her hands and knees and, reaching

111

back between her thighs, found Reggie's erection.

"Ease in," she whispered. "Gently now."

Reggie felt her hand wrap around his shaft and guide him to the entrance to her womb. Jessie's head was against the grass, her hair spread out like a golden fan across the grass.

Her ass, white, full, and tender was beneath his hands as she drew him in still farther. The sun had warmed her flesh and it danced in her hair. Reggie plunged himself in to the hilt, feeling her tender flesh surround him. He threw back his head and laughed out loud.

Jessie could feel her lover shift and sway and stroke against her, feel his hands kneading her buttocks, feel his body arch and then suddenly fill her with warmth, and she sagged against the ground, her own quaking climax sending tremors of pleasure through her.

Without losing him she rolled onto her back and drew Reggie down, locking her feet together behind his waist, kissing his mouth greedily as he lay against her, dozing contentedly.

Jessie was ready to awaken him, to nip at his shoulder with her teeth, to run her finger down the cleft of his ass, to gently squeeze him and bring him awake—and then she heard the sound of a horse where none belonged.

She lay there for a minute, Reggie's weight against her. It was tricky but she rolled him on his side, waited until she was sure he was sound asleep again, and then she rose.

She rose, snatching up her blouse and the Colt .38 pistol. There was a horse there, where none belonged, and that meant trouble in her mind.

Why she wanted to let Reggie sleep she wasn't sure, but she did and it turned out to be the best decision.

Jessie rose and walked silently across the clearing, wearing only her blouse. Her bottom, white and perfect, showed beneath her shirttail. In her hand the slate-gray Colt gleamed dully.

The sun was clear and bright, the air rich with the scent of grass and flowers. In the pines it was cool and dark. In the pines where the sound of the horse had led Jessica Starbuck.

It was silent then, only a jay squawking in the distant trees broke the silence. But the sound of the horse came again and Jessie moved toward the gray bluff before her.

She crept through a stand of cedar trees and over stacks of gray, moss-stained boulders before she found the cave. And in the cave the horse and armor.

# Chapter 11

Jessica paused at the entrance. Sunlight allowed her to see the armor stacked to one side of the cave, to pick out the gigantic black horse beyond.

The horse stood in a carefully made stall watching Jessie who worked her way toward him, seeing the tack, the horse's armor plate, the silver-mounted saddle.

Jessica reached the stall and rested a hand on the great horse's shoulder. The sleek obsidian hide twitched at her touch.

"Easy there, big boy," Jessie said softly. "What are you doing here, huh?"

She had her suspicions, but she tried not to believe them. Reggie had brought her here. Reggie—the one who had his secret hideaways, the one Ki had met late at night in the stable, the one who said he had something new to show her, something private and very secret.

Like the black knight's horse?

115

If that wasn't the answer, what was? Why hide a horse here in the hills? Jessie didn't think it was the time to ask Reggie. He would only smile disarmingly and come up with something plausible.

She carefully backed out of the cave and returned to the grassy ledge, stepping into trousers and boots as Reggie stirred and sat up.

"Been walking?" he asked, rubbing his head sleepily.

"Yes."

He must have heard something in her voice, for he came alert and watched her for a moment with intentness. He rose then, catlike, and dressed in silence. Jessie watched him, trying not to believe he was the black knight, the cartel operative.

"Ready to go back?" he asked. He smiled as he came to her, took her shoulders, and kissed her throat. "There's an ox being roasted, a lot of wine ready to be poured. A hero's feast will be served tonight."

"And in the morning the hero will be dead."

Reggie shrugged as if his own life had little importance. Or maybe he was just that self-confident. Maybe he didn't believe he could be killed.

"It doesn't seem to make a lot of sense, I know—"

Jessie spat back, *"Doesn't seem to!* You know it doesn't. Look at your father throwing away a lifetime's savings on this castle. And you, the other knights—as you call yourselves—willing to die for entertainment. Or maybe you see yourselves as some great manly warrior, I don't know. Yes, it is something I can't understand. It makes no sense at all, and you know it."

"It's the way they want it," was all Reggie said.

"That's the way you want it—possibly to die out there?"

"We die, every one of us, when the time comes."

Jessica just gave up the argument. She asked him a dif-

116

ferent sort of question. "Who are the Teutonic Knights?"

"What? Oh, just a group of men who share father's hobby."

"Prussians?" Jessie asked. Reggie had started to swing aboard his horse. Now he stopped halfway up and just stared at the blonde.

"I think so," he answered. "Yes."

"Haven't you met them before?"

"No. They correspond with father, I think. This Von Rundstedt did, at least."

"He'll murder that kid, that Joseph Cavanaugh."

"Joey? He won't be killed," Reggie answered with a laugh, settling into his saddle. "The worst that will happen is he'll get knocked silly and be mighty pleased with himself for having won his spurs."

"And become a man?"

"If you like," Reggie said. "Look, Jessica, most cultures have rites in which a boy becomes a man, accepts his responsibilities. Ours doesn't. Maybe we should have had some such rite."

"Maybe. I just wonder what kind of men you make with your rites."

Then she fell silent. She was too frustrated just then to handle conversation. Frustrated with the inability to pin down the black knight, to prove that the Teutonic Knights were cartel men, to protect the Utes, or to stop this damned bloody game of the Whitechapels!

The people from Camden and many from Sharpsville had started to arrive. Some family men with wives and kids, but mostly cowboys, lumbermen, prospectors, looking for excitement and a cheap drunk.

They'd come to the right place.

Ki had been watching them arrive all morning. It was going to be a warm, bright afternoon and a long night. Ki

117

knew only one man of those whom he saw—Barge Haycox. Perhaps the gunman had been given a second chance to kill Ki.

"Much excitement," the voice behind Ki said and he turned slowly, knowing from the accent who it was.

"Much excitement, much trouble," Ki told Sato.

"Yes," the squat Japanese said, moving forward to stand beside Ki in the shadow of the castle wall. From there they could see the arrivals, see the gay tents with their colored pennants flying, hear the banjo picking.

Sato said, "What a country, Ki. These people—ignorant and drunken, crude."

"They are only people. You said the same thing once about the peasants in Japan," Ki recalled.

"But this rabble..." Sato waved a disparaging hand. "What do you see in this culture, Ki? Why are you here? Is it the blond woman?"

"Be careful, Sato, I warn you," Ki said very slowly.

Sato made a disgusted sound with his lips. "Such a country!" he said.

"And what brings you here?"

"What? The tournament! Only the tournament offers civilization, refinement, culture."

"Warrior culture," Ki said, looking toward the hills. He could see two horses returning. Jessie was all right, then. He worried about her. Reginald Whitechapel was hardly above suspicion.

"Yes, warrior culture. I am samurai!" Sato began loudly thumping his own chest.

"Please, I have heard these remarks before," Ki interrupted. "The way of the samurai is dead. Can you not admit it? You are in the midst of a dying culture."

"Are you not a warrior?" Sato challenged.

118

"A different sort of warrior."

"Yes, but you fight," Sato said, eyes narrowing. He tapped Ki on the shoulder for emphasis, something Ki didn't like a bit. "You fight, too, old friend."

"Now," Ki said slowly, "you have chosen the wrong word, Sato-san."

"Are we not friends, Ki?" the short man said, spreading his arms.

"How can we be friends? Have I forgotten?" Ki retorted.

Sato laughed. "Have I? Have I forgotten that I swore that when we next met one of us would die?" The humor, the facade of amiability was gone now. Sato was a samurai once again. "I have made the vow and I will keep it."

"Go fight your armored knights," Ki said with disgust. "I wasn't trained to fight for entertainment."

"Nor was I. I was trained to fight to kill . . . and *te* will not stand long before my sword, Ki. I assure you of that. When it is over, this tournament, you and I shall duel and we shall see what the bare hand can do against the samurai."

"Excuse me," Ki said. Then he strode away, and even from ten paces he could hear the sharp, angry expulsion of breath from the man who would kill him.

Ki nearly walked into Von Rundstedt. The big Prussian turned dark, emotionless eyes on Ki, said nothing, and strolled on with several of his henchmen behind him.

Jessica was near enough to see Ki's wave now and she turned her horse toward him, saying farewell to Reggie, who glanced toward Ki and nodded.

"Any progress?" Jessica asked as she reached Ki. She swung down, slightly breathless, from her horse.

Ki shook his head negatively. "None, unless you count another death threat as progress," he answered stonily.

"What is it, Ki?" She took his arm, and they walked the

119

periphery of the fair. They saw quite a few men who had already managed to get drunk. They would never last through to the events of combat.

"Sato."

"Who is he, anyway?" Jessie asked.

"A man from a long time ago. Before I was . . . before I left Japan."

Jessica looked into Ki's eyes, but she could see she wasn't going to get the entire story, not even now. "He's a samurai, isn't he?"

"So he calls himself. He was raised in that discipline. He was the hireling of a great lord, Jessie, a lord who was known for his cruelty."

"Yes?"

Ki lifted his eyes to the hills. "Sato was hired to protect the lord's life. He failed."

"Someone killed him."

"So it seems. He was a dirty man who needed to be killed, and he was killed," Ki said.

"And Sato believes he knows who did it."

"And Sato," Ki answered, *"knows* who did it. It was a disgrace to him and his masters that such a thing happened. He was obviously not retained as a bodyguard to the lord's family."

"Ki?" Jessie stopped and turned Ki to face her. "Will he kill you?"

"Yes, assuredly. If he gets the chance, Jessie, Sato will kill me."

"That's all we need," Jessie said after a minute. Ki smiled a little grimly.

"Yes. What a life we live! If honor did not demand that we continue, sometimes I think—"

Jessie said, "Honor does demand it. For me. We are

120

talking about the people who killed my mother and father, Ki."

"Yes. Yes, that is so. And for me honor also demands that we finish this dreadful job."

"All right—what can we do about Sato?" she asked with a strong exhalation.

"About Sato, nothing. That is my problem. What else have we learned this day? Reggie—who is he? The man we believe him to be or not?"

"I don't know. Damn it all, Ki, I still don't know if he's the dark knight. I don't know who he is or what he is. If he's not the man behind all of this, I can't figure why he's acting the way he is. Why have a horse hidden away in the hills? Why ride in at night through a secret entrance? Why does a healthy, seemingly normal, young man live like this— out here, away from everything? There doesn't seem to be any explanation for Reggie's behavior but a criminal one."

"What does your heart tell you, Jessie?" Ki asked.

She was silent, hesitant. "My heart tells me he's a good man."

"Well, then, let's not jump to a conclusion."

"Yes," Jessica responded.

Evening came in early, but the meadow stayed bright. Torches lit up the sky. Songs filled the air. Drunks lay in shadow, dragged up against the wall of the castle.

Inside the roasted ox was served to the knights who were in their finery. Jessica wore a long green dress cut very low to reveal most of her tender white breasts—Reggie had dug the dress up somewhere. It fit perfectly and was definitely appealing to the men.

Even Von Rundstedt who seemed to be a mechanical man couldn't keep his eyes off her.

121

Ethelbert Whitechapel was holding forth, his tongue stimulated by too much wine. "Why these peasants ought to be allowed to roam the grounds is beyond me."

"Tradition," Sir John replied.

Ethelbert might not have heard him. "Scurvy things. Peasants. They have their courage in their holsters. If it weren't for Colonel Colt, they'd be afraid to walk the streets of their own little town."

"I don't think that's quite fair, Ethelbert," Sir John said.

"Fair?" The red-headed knight flushed angrily. "Why do I have to be fair to these savages! What are they but illiterate layabouts? In certain, more advanced countries, they'd be herded to work camps and that would be that. They'd be of some use to civilization then, wouldn't they, Von Rundstedt?" Ethelbert demanded.

"I do not know," Von Rundstedt said, his accent guttural, his eyes lowered.

"Of course you do." Ethelbert persisted, but the Prussian wouldn't be drawn into the conversation. He continued to glower at Ethelbert who looked at his hand holding the wine cup. Then he slowly lowered the cup, rose, and dabbed at his lips.

"Excuse me," Ethelbert said, "I'm not feeling well and tomorrow is the tournament."

They watched as he staggered backward, nearly tipping over his heavy chair, and walked toward the stairs across the hall.

Von Rundstedt looked at Jessie and smiled the most unnatural and indecent smile she'd ever seen. Then, the meal continued.

When there was nothing left but wine and boasting of old triumphs, Jessica and Ki excused themselves. It was already late as they made their way upstairs.

"Be careful tonight," Ki said to her.

"I'm always careful."

"Yes, but perhaps not careful enough. Something will happen now, Jessie. Perhaps tonight, perhaps tomorrow. The cartel must be out of patience with the game they have been playing. They must be out of patience with us."

"Yes." Jessica had to agree. Soon now this would come to a head. Soon they would have to be eliminated if the cartel were to continue its greedy plan to take over the White River Basin.

And still they hadn't found the leverage they needed to fight back properly, hadn't found any trustworthy allies—the law in this part of the country was nothing more than a farce.

And still they hadn't stopped the black knight's raids.

Ki said good night to Jessica at her door and listened until he heard her turn the heavy key to lock the door. He then made his way back to his own room.

He opened the door and stepped quickly to one side in a defensive position. He wasn't alone in the darkness.

"C'mon now, Mr. Ki," Carrie said from his bed. "Don't be shy. It's only me. Let's have a laugh or two, shall we?"

It seemed like a fair idea. Ki stepped from his pants and went to her, falling into her warm embrace.

# Chapter 12

There was trouble beyond the door—and the castle was a dark and haunted fortress—but behind the door, in the bed with the freshly ironed linen, with the loving, soft woman there wasn't a thing in the universe to worry about. There was only Carrie and her mouth, her gentle hands, her womanhood.

"Hold it there, Ki. Ah—you devil, you fine man, now a little stroke and another . . . ah, you devil!" she said loudly. She reached out and dragged Ki's head down to her breasts, holding it there as he tasted her sweetness.

"A little farther, Ki, another push," she said and then she shuddered, sighing into his ear. "That's good, so good."

She began to come apart then. Her hands clutched at Ki's groin, at his solid ramrod, at his shoulders, as Carrie became a rolling, pitching thing thumping her pelvis against his. Her mouth opened in silent pleasured agony.

Ki was hard put to keep pace. His hands, knowing and

125

gentle, found her nipples, dropped between her legs to touch her where he entered her. His lips traced patterns across her throat and face and Carrie murmured, "You are so gentle, so good. So..."

Whatever else he was Ki was never to know as Carrie found a sudden blissful climax. Ki, lifting her with his hands, thrust against her time and again as she thrashed back and forth. He found his own rushing completion.

She lay there, sated and soft, heavy with satisfaction. Ki was beside her and she let her finger run along his jawline, trace his lips.

"What will I do when you go, Mr. Ki? Lord, what will I ever do?"

Ki kissed her. He had an idea Carrie would make out well enough after he was gone.

"I'm happy," she said, "that you're not one of those madmen, one of those knights as they call themselves. I'd have to worry about you then, wouldn't I?"

"Yes. I am happy you don't have to worry," Ki answered.

"Me, too. It's not like you're going to put on an iron suit and go out there in the morning and maybe get killed," she said.

"No," Ki answered, "it's not like that at all." But it was exactly like that—he would wear no iron suit but there was little time left. The cartel would have to make its move and its first move would be to eliminate Jessie and Ki.

There was no point in explaining all of that to Carrie who snuggled nearer to him in the cool night, lifted her warm thigh, and threw it over Ki's leg. She lay there softly snoring, a small thing in her own small world. Ki kissed her gently on the forehead and then lay back to lie sleeplessly watching the stars through the slit window.

Dawn flushed the sky beyond the window with orange and then crimson. Ki could hear people up and stirring and he, too, slipped from the bed.

After dressing he went out, leaving Carrie. Jessica was up when he got to her room, up and looking concerned, which briefly puzzled Ki until he recalled that a man she seemed to care a lot about was to fight in the morning tournament.

"There's a lot of activity downstairs," Ki said.

"It's been going on for hours."

"Preparations for the game."

She nodded, picking her hat up from the bed, putting it on her head.

"For the *games*," she replied.

They started downstairs, expecting to find men at the great table, eating, but it appeared a general fast was in effect.

"Still smells of roasted ox and wine," Jessie noted.

"Jessie—today will be a good time for them."

"What do you mean?" she asked, turning toward him.

"While our attention is on this combat these men are going to engage in—don't let all of your attention be on the combatants."

"All of the knights will be in armor. There's little chance of *them* sneaking up on someone."

"They will have rifles as well. They have squires, lackeys, whatever they choose to call them. I don't think we know who we can trust, Jessica. All I know is that if I were planning an assassination it would be on this busy, clamorous day. In the crowd."

Jessica mulled that over and then nodded agreement. "I'll be careful."

"Jessie," Ki said, briefly taking her hand, "I mean . . . don't trust anyone."

"Not even Reggie, you mean."

"That's exactly what I mean. If they want the White

127

River Basin, they'll have to take it soon or their camouflage is no good. They'll have to do it now. Today or tonight at the latest. They'll not want us around."

Jessica was her father's daughter. She said grimly, "I don't care what they *want*. They've got us and the only way to get rid of us is to kill us. I don't think they're good enough to do that."

"No..." Ki smiled faintly. "Only don't underestimate them. They haven't built a worldwide empire by being inefficient or timid."

By the time they went outside into the dawn the fair, the newly constructed lists, the long valley were all alive with people. Drunken cowboys, Indians, lumbermen, curiosity seekers, lovers of sport, gamblers. Picnic blankets had been set up on the grass so that children would have a good view of the combat to come.

The banjo picker, joined by a man with red whiskers and a big brass tuba, marched through the fair playing loudly if not too proficiently.

As Jessica and Ki emerged from the gates, there was another blaring musical sound. Looking up to the castle walls, they saw two trumpeters in medieval costume and a minute later heard and saw the procession moving out of the castle and to the field.

In full armor Sir Whitechapel led the parade. Behind him was his squire. Then came Ethelbert, Reggie, and Joseph Cavanaugh. Following were Waldo the Rumanian, Seth, Sir Peter, and Lord George Austin with their squires.

Last were the Teutonic Knights, their armor black, their black horses bright with silver and crimson trappings.

They made a slow circuit of the grounds while the local men gawked, shouted, or ran after them. It was all very exciting—it was time for someone to die.

Jessie walked past the striped tents to the head of the

lists. Reggie was there, pulling on his mailed gloves. He watched her approach, unsmiling.

"I didn't think you'd want to be here," he said, tugging his chain hood on and adjusting it while his squire buckled his greaves around his shins.

"Sure," she shrugged. "Why not?"

"You didn't seem real taken with the idea."

"It stinks . . . but I'm here." She pulled a scarf from her pocket. "In the books I've read the knight always wore his lady's colors."

"Yes." Reggie smiled and took the pale blue scarf. "He does."

There was a roll of drums and the sound of trumpets. Jessie glanced toward the long scarlet lists. "Who is it?" she wanted to know. "Who's first?"

"Ethelbert, I think. And Waldo."

"You don't seem concerned one way or the other."

A little tense, he said, "I'm thinking about my own chances, Jessie, not about my uncle."

"Well—" she got to tiptoe and kissed him. "Good luck, since you won't be reasonable and forget all this childish bloody business."

"I can't . . . I just can't," Reggie said and there was something in his tone that escaped Jessie. He shook his head and turned away, letting his squire who stood on a block of wood fit his visored helmet.

Jessica made her way to the grandstand where Sir White-chapel sat looking flushed and proud and eager.

"Please, my dear," the old man said, "sit beside me."

"All right. Have you seen Ki?"

"I haven't seen him. Sit up here now, my dear."

"I should find Ki."

"He'll be here, I imagine. Sit." He patted her hand and strained forward. "It's about to begin. At last. My first

129

tournament. God, how I wish that I . . ."

He didn't finish his thought. The first two combatants were lining up in the lists, opposing each other down the long parallel runways. The chargers sidestepped uneasily as the squires pushed them into position. A buzz of anticipation ran through the crowd as they ate and drank, called out to each other, and moved closer to where the gore would be.

"That's Ethelbert with the blue trappings," Whitechapel said. "They suppose he's overmatched against the Rumanian, but I know my stepbrother, know him well enough."

There was a roar from the crowd as the two helmeted knights charged suddenly toward each other, lances leveled, horses' manes and tails flying, dust swirling skyward.

It was over in seconds. Ethelbert's blunted lance scored a direct hit on Waldo's shield and the Rumanian was slammed from his horse and into the list to lie there a jumble of darkly gleaming armor.

His squire and attendants came running to help him up. He finally did get to his feet unsteadily, removing his helmet to show a pale, blood-smeared face. Waldo lifted a hand to Ethelbert and staggered away, held up by his men.

"For that he came all the way from Rumania," Jessica said with wonder.

"Yes. Magnificent, wasn't it? The shock when they collide! Magnificent!" Whitechapel was rocking back and forth on his chair. There was a bit of spittle in the corner of his mouth. His cheeks were deeply flushed.

Maybe he was getting his money's worth. And how much had this all cost him? Jessie wondered.

"The next pairing," Whitechapel said eagerly.

Jessica lifted green eyes to the lists. Sir Peter was facing Seth of Burgundy now. Both men gleamed in their armor and colors. The wind moved the cloth tied to Seth's helmet.

They started forward suddenly, charging down the lists as a cheer went up from the crowd. They came together with a clash like thunderous cymbals. Seth's lance shattered and he fell into Peter's side of the lists, nearly to be trampled by the armored horse the Englishman rode. He was very slow in getting up even with his armor removed by his squires.

Two of the Teutonic Knights faced each other next. Black and crimson, faces hidden behind visors. Whitechapel leaned farther forward in his chair, biting at his knuckles. Jessie looked away. A sane person could only stand so much of this.

She couldn't see Reggie just then and Ki still hadn't arrived. And just where were they? The roar of the crowd brought Jessie's eyes up as the two knights rushed toward each other, lances levelled.

Ki also glanced toward the lists and he cursed, hurrying madly on.

There wasn't much time, maybe not enough. A rifleman was on the castle wall and he was sighting his Winchester toward the grandstand where Jessica sat watching the tournament.

Ki had just happened to glance up, his eye perhaps drawn by movement where none should have been. Sunlight gleaming on metal had focused his concentration on the rifleman who was stretched out behind the parapet, aiming at the tournament onlookers.

And Ki knew instantly which onlooker was the sniper's target. Or he *feared* he did.

Jessica Starbuck.

Ki rushed on. Crossing the drawbridge, he heard the roar from the crowd, saw the two Teutonic Knights start their charge. Then Ki was inside the castle walls, taking the outside steps five and six at a time, believing that he knew when the sniper would fire.

When the two knights collided, the crashing sound was enough to cover almost any noise. That and the subsequent cheer should cover the crack of a distant rifle shot.

And there wasn't going to be enough time until that happened; there just wasn't.

Ki's breath came in ragged gasps. The *shuriken* was cold and sharp in his hand. His legs seemed to move in slow motion no matter how he urged them to leap the stone stairs.

It all happened at once. The knights came together and Ki, emerging on the parapet, threw his *shuriken* without pausing to think about the act, without consciously taking aim. The rifleman fired and a puff of smoke rose from the barrel.

Ki cried out, but his cry was lost in the roar of the crowd below.

The rifleman turned, staggered backward, slapped at the shuriken embedded in his neck, and toppled from the parapet.

Ki rushed to the parapet and stared at the grandstand, his heart in his throat. If she had been hurt . . . but she hadn't been. No one below seemed to be aware that anything had even happened. All eyes had been on the jousting and not on the wall.

Ki hadn't been in time to stop the rifleman from firing his weapon, but he'd been in time to make his aim go astray.

"That, my friend," Ki said to himself, "is far too close for comfort."

Shaking his head, he wiped back his dark hair and started down the stairs. He found the sniper partially in the moat. His face, bruised and lacerated, was showing.

Ki bit at the inside of his cheek, shook his head, and

132

after looking around, kicked Barge Haycox or what was left of him into the moat.

"He just didn't manage to live up to his reputation," Ki said. He watched Haycox slip away and then started for the grandstand. He missed the joust between Lord Austin and one of the Teutonic Knights. Austin's head was nearly ripped from his body by a blunt lance, he was told later.

He managed to reach the grandstand as Reggie, sitting on a black charger, made his run at the Teutonic Knight he had drawn. It was a skillful exhibition. Reggie's lance unseated the man violently and he paraded his horse past the grandstand, Whitechapel rising to cheer, Jessica sitting tensely.

Only when Reggie was gone did Jessie seem to notice Ki. "And where have you been hiding?" she asked.

"There's too much bloodshed down here," Ki said with a straight face. Jessie frowned. She knew Ki well enough to know that there was something behind his words.

"There's going to be more," she said and Ki looked up to see Von Rundstedt taking his position. At the other end of the lists was the young man, Joseph Cavanaugh.

It seemed forever before they started, but when they did, it was with thunder and fury. It was obvious right away that Cavanaugh was nervous, unsettled. He didn't have his charger under control and he failed to tuck his lance away properly. It wavered as they came through the lists.

Von Rundstedt saw it all. He must have known better than any of them that his opponent was unprepared, barely tested, but it didn't slow the Teuton down. His lance caught Cavanaugh in the center of his breastplate. Cavanaugh was unseated savagely, and when he fell it was obvious to everyone that he wasn't going to get up quickly.

He didn't get up at all. Reggie, without his greaves and

helmet, was one of the first to Joseph's side. It didn't take him long to discover the broken neck. He stood and shook his head.

"Well," Sir John Whitechapel murmured, "too bad. Only the first round, too." And then he sat down to wait for the second round.

# Chapter 13

Jessica Starbuck couldn't stand it. "You've got to stop this bloody show," she told Whitechapel. "A man's been killed!"

"Stop it?" Whitechapel gawked at her as if she had lost her mind. "This is what they have all come here for. *This* is what I have built the castle for, why I have come to America. This is what the people out there have come to see. Stop it? Not likely. The mountains have never seen the likes of this before and they'll never see it again. Besides, young lady, the knights wouldn't tolerate it. Two years they wait between combat trials. Two years preparing and training. Would you ask them to throw all of that away?"

"A man is dead," Jessie said again, very slowly.

Whitechapel was out of patience. "Now you sound like that damned interfering Scotland Yard. Reason I left England in the first place. Civilized! They think they're civilized—like you, I take it. *Civilized!* And what good is that if the flavor, the fire, the color is gone from life, I ask you?

Live without chance, without risk—you might live longer, but it's not worth the living, my dear Miss Starbuck."

There wasn't much to say to that tirade. Jessie looked at Ki who shook his head. Sato had just entered the lists and they watched as he met and handily defeated a Teutonic Knight with no apparent injury to either.

"Von Rundstedt," Ki said. He was looking at the dark, square Prussian who, helmetless, stood glaring at the Teuton who was just unseated. "He doesn't like to lose. He wants to be the victor always. He won't tolerate a loser. I wouldn't want to be in that poor beggar's shoes."

The second round began after a noon break during which the knights rested or watered their horses or ate or drank depending on their inclinations. Joseph Cavanaugh was carried away to the dark, cold dungeon to await his burial.

In the second pairings Von Rundstedt drew one of his own men. He finished the man off as ruthlessly as he had finished Cavanaugh, except that the Teutonic Knight was luckier. He survived.

Sato had Sir Peter and he unseated the Englishman on the second charge after each man had broken his first lance.

Ethelbert displayed some skill in nearly decapitating his Teutonic opponent with his lance. The padded tip caught the knight under the helmet, lifting him bodily from his horse's back. He was lucky he didn't break his neck, and he managed to get up.

"Good show, Ethelbert, very good, excellent!" Sir John Whitechapel clapped his hands together like an excited kid and rose to his feet. His eyes were wide, eager. He sat rigid, hunched forward between collisions of mounted men, and at the moment of impact, when the armored knights came together, he trembled as if in orgasm.

Ki was with Jessica in the grandstand as the second round

played out and the afternoon wore on. There was a lot of time between rounds spent watching tumblers and acrobats and listening to musicians.

"There is only one combat left," Ki said.

"Yes," Jessica answered, "I know it."

Reggie. And just how did she feel about Reggie now? They had discussed it briefly between rounds but came to no conclusion. "He was with me, Ki, when the Ute fields were burned the last time!"

"Was he? And the other night when I followed the dark knight back to the castle, it was Reggie in the stable with the hard-ridden horse."

"That could have been coincidence."

"If you say it was, then it was," Ki said, bowing out of the conversation, sensing that he was not going to sway Jessica now.

"Well, Ki . . .?"

She implored him to agree with her, to believe that Reggie was innocent. Ki lifted his chin toward the head of the lists.

"They are coming out now."

Jessie sighed and looked away. On his black charger, Reggie was entering the lists, being given the lance by his squire. The Teutonic Knight he faced had a cylindrical helmet and wore dark purple and black silks over his armor. They had seen the man before, seen him beat Lord George Austin handily.

Whitechapel was nearly beside himself, wriggling in his seat, biting at his knuckles.

"He's getting his money's worth, " Ki said.

"Perhaps all it will cost him is a son," Jessie responded bitterly.

The knights were off, charging full tilt down the lists. Reggie had his lance high and now he lowered it, bracing himself as the two men clashed, armor ringing, dust rolling skyward, a horse crying out in surprise.

When the dust settled, Reginald Whitechapel, Jessica's scarf still tied around his upper arm, rode off, leaving the Teutonic Knight in the dust. Ki glanced at Whitechapel, who was flushed with triumph, with pride.

He looked then at Jessica who was pale, just a little shaken. She did not like this game.

"And that leaves the four of them," Ki said. "Tomorrow they will be reduced to two, and then a man will die so that another can be named champion."

She looked at him miserably, a little angrily, Ki thought. She hadn't wanted or needed that pointed out to her.

Sato, Von Rundstedt, Ethelbert, and Reggie were the ones left. Two would be eliminated in the morning and then the padding would be removed from the lances. Then unseating your opponent would not be enough. Then the broadswords would be sharpened, and if the opportunity offered itself, they would be used.

"How can we lose now?" Whitechapel exulted, coming to his feet. "How can we lose? Two chances! Ethelbert and Reggie."

Ki asked, "And if it comes down to those two, Sir Whitechapel, how can you *win?*"

The Englishman had no answer for that. He looked vaguely perplexed as if surprised that Ki's mind could work in such a way.

What did it matter if his son or brother were killed? Sir John's look seemed to say. Didn't they understand? He would have the champion!


It was Carrie who gave Ki further bad news. She caught him by the arm as he entered the castle, leaving the noise, the banjo picking, the drumming, the trumpeting, the drunken hooting behind.

"Did you see the young man, Mr. Ki? Did he find you?"

"What young man?" Ki asked, glancing at Jessica. Carrie was upset; that was obvious.

"The redhead, the farm boy. Name of Wertz, I believe."

"No. What did he want?"

"Well, he brought the dead man up for one thing."

"What dead man!"

"Janky . . . Yankowert?"

"Jankowitz?" Ki asked.

"Yes, that is the name, Mr. Ki. There was no doctor at Sharpsville, but he'd heard we might have one up this way— not that it mattered. The other one was dead long before he got here."

"Where is he now—Wertz, I mean?" Ki demanded.

"With the dead man." She nodded toward the dungeon, her expression darkening. "Down there."

"Coming?" Ki asked Jessica.

"Try stopping me."

They went down the long stairway to the dungeon where two slabs, side by side, held the inert bodies of Joseph Cavanaugh and the rancher, Al Jankowitz. Wertz was standing nearby looking helpless and dazed. He looked up as Jessie and Ki came forward.

"Hello," he said.

"Hello, Wertz. What happened?"

"I don't know." The boy shrugged. "They came and hit us and then I thought there was a doctor at Camden. Thought you were up here . . . I don't know."

He wasn't real coherent. Ki slowed him down. "All right, who hit you?"

"Don't know. Bunch of men."

"How many?"

"Ten, twelve. Burned the house and the new barn," Wertz said. "I tried to fight 'em, but I knew I couldn't hold out.

I lit out, crossed the creek underwater, and got into the woods."

"Damn it all," Ki said.

"Wasn't your fault," Wertz said.

"Wasn't it?" Ki asked but Wertz didn't hear him. "What happened then? How'd you find Jankowitz?"

"How?" The kid wiped dried blood from his eyebrow and looked at it. Then he shook himself mentally and told Ki, "First, I went north but when I saw the Hicks place had been burned down—"

"The Hicks place?"

"Yeah. I didn't see Hicks, but I guess maybe he had gone to join up with his wife and daughter. He sent them out the day before."

"That's something."

"Yeah, well, then I thought about Jankowitz being alone down there like he was. I didn't feel much like going back, I guarantee you, but I did. Found him shot up pretty good. His house had been burned as well. Stock run off. It's the end of us, I guess." He looked at the dead man again. "Maybe I'm lucky, I don't know. I keep thinking of what my father told me before he died. Remember, Ki? 'Stand tall.'"

"I remember."

"Think I let him down?" Wertz asked, lifting his eyes and then letting them slide away.

"No." Ki briefly touched the kid's shoulder. "I don't think anyone could've stood much taller."

"The ranch is gone," the boy said miserably.

"You'll get it back."

"And the stock? How? These men riding around here in their armor—one of them is the man behind this, isn't he?"

"We think so," Jessie answered.

"Which one?"

Jessica shook her head. "We don't know. When we do find out—"

"When you do find out," Wertz interrupted hotly. "You *kill* him. Kill him!"

And then he couldn't stand it anymore and he turned away to sob, his great shoulders quaking with the tears. Jessie touched Ki's arm and they turned to walk up the stairs.

Outside it was dusk, orange and deep purple in the skies. They couldn't enjoy the beauty of the evening a bit.

"It was my fault," Ki said.

"No."

"I should have realized that the time was right for striking at the ranchers."

Jessie said, "You couldn't have anymore than I could have. If you are to blame, then I am equally at fault."

Ki wasn't listening. A man had died and he felt responsible. "Any fool could have predicted that this was the time to make the attacks on the white ranchers. The cartel wasn't holding those gunmen back for no purpose. While Jessica and Ki were watching the tournament—yes, that is the time."

"But, Ki—"

"And, of course, they had planned to kill us both while the tournament was in progress—while we were distracted, while Ki was—"

"What do you mean, Ki? Was there an attempt to kill us?" Jessie asked.

Ki smiled very thinly. "Yes, there was," and he told her about Barge Haycox finally.

"No one's even found the body!"

"Or mentioned it."

"Oh, Ki," Jessie showed genuine frustration for the first time. "What are we going to do? I can't recall a job where we've taken so many wrong turns."

He was still mulling her question—what *would* they do next? They could afford no more wrong turns. Ki thought he knew what had to be done.

"The white ranchers have been run off. All three ranches have been destroyed. Only young Wertz and the Hicks family remain alive. Hicks, quite rightly, quite wisely, has taken his family to Sharpsville."

"Yes?" Jessie prompted as Ki continued to think aloud.

"And so there is only one target left for the cartel," Ki concluded.

"The Utes."

"Yes. The Utes must be driven from their land. And there is no more time. The tournament is nearly over. There will be no more reason for knights to appear in these hills. Besides"—Ki said this after long consideration—"the man behind this may be dead tomorrow, Jessica. He cannot allow *that*."

"The man behind it?"

"Think of it. Tomorrow the four knights continue their battles. Who are they? Von Rundstedt, the Teuton. Reggie whose history is suspicious. Ethelbert who is a murky man perhaps deprived of his inheritance. Sato—Sato who is a warrior by craft, Sato who has fought for profit many times, offering his services to the emperor, to the lord, to the cartel?" Ki watched the sunset above the Rockies for a minute longer. "One of these must be the figure behind the cartel's scheme—or don't you agree?"

Jessica had no ready answer. One of them, it seemed, must be the dark knight, the leader of the plot to take over the White River Basin. And as Ki had deduced that man would have to take the chance of being killed in combat in the morning.

Such a man would never take that chance.

"It isn't Reggie," was all Jessie said finally. Ki just looked at her. After a few moments she added, "They will strike tonight. With all the force at their command."

Ki didn't think that would be necessary. "Why use fifty men when a half dozen might do the trick?" he asked.

"The Teutonic Knights?"

"Maybe." Ki was cautious. He hadn't done real well thinking things out to this point.

"But you think so, don't you? You think that it's Von Rundstedt we want and that his knights could storm through the Ute village, driving them all away. A single dark knight might not do it, hasn't done it to this point, but many dark knights, many *conquistadores* returning, bringing the curse of fire and death—well, that might very well do the job. And if the Utes leave voluntarily—what else could it be called if they pull out due to superstition?—and the white ranchers fail to return . . . then the job is done, isn't it?"

"Then," Ki agreed somberly, "the job is done. It must be tonight. It must be a strike against the Utes. And we, Jessica, must stop it."

"And we, Ki, will stop it."

# Chapter 14

It was black and cold. The moon hadn't yet lifted its head above the horizon and the going was slow along the difficult trail. Jessie and Ki rode silently for the most part. It wouldn't do to have undue noise this night. It was time for the last battle of the White River Basin to begin, and they both knew it as they knew that if this battle were lost to the cartel, so was the war lost.

They found the Ute camp at eleven and they walked their horses slowly through it, looking right and left, seeing no one, but noting the signs of departure. Packs made up, horses drawn in close to the camp, travois prepared.

They found Chi-Tha in an obstinate mood. He came from his wickiup to stand before them with something approaching belligerence. "You are back, you man from across the sea. The white girl, too."

"We are here."

"This is no place for you. Why don't you go?" the old man said.

"Because we must talk. We have come with a warning for you and you must take heed."

Jessie swung down and Ki followed her. Chi-Tha watched them with suspicion. They walked to the old man; this time he didn't invite them into his home. He had seen enough of strangers and spirits.

"What is it?" He spoke tonelessly.

"The men in armor are coming tonight," Jessica said. "We're almost sure of it."

*"Men?* Now there will be more than one spirit?"

"Now there will be more than one," Jessie said, "but Chi-Tha, you must listen to us, these are not spirits!"

"They are," the old Ute said obstinately.

"They are not!" Jessie, who could be as obstinate as anyone, said passionately. "They are men, living men who covet your land."

"White ranchers?" Chi-Tha said in doubtful tones.

"Not the whites you know. Other men from far away."

"Yes." Chi-Tha answered as if Ki and Jessica were children who could not possibly understand the truth of things.

"Chi-Tha," Jessica went on insistently, "surely your people have seen the whites camped in the hills. When you are hunting, you must run across them."

"Perhaps we have seen some men. But they have not bothered us," the Ute leader said.

"But they will. Don't you see? That's why they are gathered there, to force you from your land. They have used the old legend to try to frighten you, and if that fails, then they will use modern methods, guns."

"Then we will fight," Chi-Tha answered. Living men with guns were a different story.

"Then you had better get ready," Ki said, "because they will be coming."

"When?"

"In minutes, hours? Tonight—it will be tonight."

Chi-Tha looked doubtful. There was starlight in his old, alert eyes. "Why have you come here?" he asked. "Because you are our friends?"

"No," Jessica said, sensing the old man wanted honesty, "because they are our enemies."

He studied her face in the darkness for a long minute. "There was always trouble for us before when we fought the whites."

"There won't be any trouble this time," Jessica promised him. "Not with them coming to your land to start trouble."

"I don't like this," Chi-Tha said slowly.

"I don't like it, either," Ki responded, "but that is the way things are. Men will come tonight. Their intention is to take away your land. They've already raided the three white ranchers and burned their houses."

"White against white."

"And white against Ute. This is a war for the entire basin, Chi-Tha. It is a war no one asked for, but it's come to you and now you have to decide what you will do, fight or run."

Ki's voice was deliberately taunting. Chi-Tha's warrior's pride was stung by the remark, stung by the thought that he might run from trouble. To run from a ghost was no shame—how can a man fight a ghost? But to run from these foreign whites who wanted their land. No, Chi-Tha would not have anyone think he would do that.

Still, Chi-Tha could not decide alone. "I shall have to summon a council."

"Then do it. Now."

"It is the middle of the night," the Ute answered. "Shall

147

I waken my council chiefs over this?" For the first time Chi-Tha seemed confused.

"They will come. They will come tonight," Ki told him again. "You have to be ready for them. What good will a council be in the morning if the raiders have burned your village and murdered your women and children?"

"I will go," Chi-Tha said, "and I will awaken them. But I will tell you this, foreigner, white woman—you had better be right. It had better be tonight that the raiders come."

"It will be," Ki said. "I'm sure of it. Now, hurry, you must be ready when they come."

Still doubtful, Chi-Tha went away, hitching his blanket up over his shoulders. Jessica watched him go. *"Are* we sure, Ki? Sure that it's tonight?"

But he didn't answer. Logic told him that it must be tonight. He *felt* it in his guts. But *sure?* "We are right," he said. "We must be right."

They withdrew from the Ute camp. Men were stirring now. They heard muttering voices, a woman complaining. They walked into the oaks beyond the camp and Jessica perched on a massive flat boulder, watching the starlight on the White River, seeing the golden haze in the eastern sky where the moon was yawning, beginning to rise.

"Which one is it, Ki? Which one is our cartel man? Which one is the dark knight?"

Ki didn't answer. He thought he knew but Jessica wouldn't have liked his conclusion.

Jessie went on, "Von Rundstedt is the obvious one, of course, but he arrived after this all began. He and Sato."

"They seemed to arrive after it had started, " Ki pointed out. "Maybe Von Rundstedt was hiding in the hills all along."

"Perhaps. Ethelbert was here certainly. Ethelbert—who seems to be a failure in business, who has to watch his

148

wealthy brother fritter away a possible inheritance."

"Yes."

"I know!" Jessie said, "You can say the same things about Reggie. He was here. He is the one who will inherit certainly."

Ki was silent. There was no point in guessing. He hoped to know by sunrise. Perhaps he would only learn when it was too late. If the Utes declined to fight, they wouldn't have much chance, he and Jessica. Not against forty or fifty men.

"We should have brought people with us," Jessie said as if reading Ki's thoughts. She removed her hat and rubbed her eyes. "It just seems that we have overlooked something, that we've done something wrong, something we could have . . ." She was suddenly alert as was Ki who spun toward the sound of footsteps on the leaves beneath the oaks.

It was Chi-Tha. "We will fight," he said. "We have no choice. Tell us what to do."

"I shall not pretend to tell a Ute warrior how to fight," Ki said with some sincerity, "but if you would allow me to make a few suggestions, I have an idea or two."

One of those ideas was to get the women and children out of the camp immediately. It wouldn't do to have anyone inside the wickiups when the raiders came through. Silently the Indian women moved out, taking the children and the old with them. They moved in the darkness and they seemed little more substantial than the shadows the moon cast.

When they were gone, Ki looked to the assembled warriors. "How many guns have we?"

"Few. A half dozen, perhaps," Chi-Tha said, "but we have bows and arrows. Our enemies have been served by these weapons before."

"Yes. One is as deadly as the other," Ki agreed, "but a

149

man must fight differently with different weapons."

"How would you have us fight on this night, foreign man?"

"In the way you know best. From ambush, from the cover of the cornfield, from the trees, from behind the rocks. These men are coming to destroy you. There is no need to show them the respect of warriors. Strike at them from hidden places, from out of the shadows of the night."

"At last, " Chi-Tha said with a smile, "we have found something to agree upon, Ki. When they come, they won't see a Ute. They will see nothing until the arrows strike them. Let them make noise with their guns. We will be silent and deadly."

"Good." Ki briefly rested a hand on the Indian's shoulder. "Let's take our places then. The moon is rising. They will strike soon I think."

"You—" Chi-Tha said to Ki, "you do not have a gun."

"No," Ki replied, "I have no gun."

"You must have a weapon," the Ute said. "Will you take this—it is my best bow, my best arrows."

"What will you fight with?"

"I have another. Will you honor me?" Chi-Tha asked.

"You honor me," Ki said. "Of course, I will take your bow. I will use it in a way that I hope will honor its maker."

Chi-Tha turned away then, and he called out to his men who dispersed into the darkness. Jessica waited beside Ki.

"Where?" she asked. "Up the trail?"

"In the trees, I think."

"Ki, if they don't come it's going to be a long night."

"If they do, Jessica, it will be much longer. These are not rabble come to fire their guns in the air and run at the first sight of their own blood. Not if I know the cartel. They are killers, professionals, men who will complete this job if they can."

150

"I know that."

"It would do no good to ask you to go into Sharpsville, would it?" Ki asked.

"Not a damn bit of good." She smiled brightly. "Show me where you want to lay the ambush. The moon's creeping higher. They'll be coming."

They went into the oaks, passing watching eyes, and took up position behind the crooked branch of a great tree. Then they settled in and watched the moon rise higher, shrink, and turn silver. Beyond the village the river rolled slowly past and its soft mutterings were the only sound in the night but for an owl somewhere in the oaks above them.

And then there was another sound.

Distant at first, faint. The rattling of iron, the click and clank of it, the heavy tread of a horse as Jessie and Ki waited, peering from behind the trees. The knight before the moon then appeared.

Jessie's breath caught. It looked enough like Reggie's painting to cause her to blink twice and shake her head. The knight, lance uplifted, walked his charger into the Ute camp, and he might have been a spirit—everyone seemed transfixed by his presence. Not a man raised up or fired at the dark armored thing.

Jessie watched as the horseman walked his charger through a wickiup, watched as the visored face turned toward them. She had her Colt in her hand, ready to fire, but she couldn't fire—damn all, was it Reggie?

Ki was unmoving as well. His eyes were narrow, watchful. He could see the plodding knight, the bright moon on the river, Jessie's eyes catching the starlight, the crouched, still figures of the Utes.

Nothing moved, no one, and Ki knew it had to be him who did it. The Utes were afraid; Jessie worried that it might be a man she didn't want to hurt.

151

He stood behind the limb, notched an arrow, and let it fly.

The Utes later said the shot was amazing; Ki knew it had more than a little luck winging with it. The knight wore a visor with eight bars, an inch or less apart. Ki hadn't seen the helmet at any of the jousts, but he remembered it from somewhere.

The arrow drove in between two of the visor bars, and the dark knight cried out with pain and fury as the arrow struck flesh.

"The eye," Ki thought. "I got him in the eye."

There wasn't time to consider it longer. The cry of pain had done something all of Ki's talking could not do. It had convinced the Utes that this was a flesh and blood creature, not a spirit. They rose up at once and filled the air with arrows.

All of these shots bounced harmlessly off the knight; still screaming with pain, he turned his rearing horse. The arrow was still embedded in the visor, but now a mailed hand snapped it off.

The Utes charged toward the knight, but that was a mistake on their part. Wanting to drag him from his horse, to tear him apart, they gave their positions away.

"Get back!" Ki shouted. "Back to your places."

They didn't listen. Wrapped up in blood lust, tribal memory, revenge, they charged across the moonlit clearing toward the injured knight.

And the guns opened up from the underbrush.

The cartel men had been well chosen. They were very good. To sneak up on the Ute camp without having been discovered was nearly miraculous, but then they had had the black knight to draw and hold the eyes, the attention of the White River Indians.

Now as the Utes rushed toward the bellowing knight,

the guns of the cartel thugs stabbed flame and cut them down. Jessie had her .38 in her hand and she fired back, seeing only muzzle flashes, darting shadows, the Utes in the moonlit clearing going down. Then the knight was riding out of there and Jessie chased him with two shots, which rang off his armor, before her Colt went dry and she had to reload.

Ki had been notching arrows, saving his shots until he saw flame from the barrels of the cartel rifles. Then his arrows flew and they were as deadly as ever. He tagged one cartel man who rose and ran wildly across the clearing, grasping at the arrow in his chest, before he fell and, after thrashing around briefly, died.

Another seemed to be a hit, but that man didn't even move. Nor did his Winchester fire again.

It was confusion on a grand scale suddenly. From the south a dozen mounted cartel men charged through the camp. Behind them came four mounted knights.

"Ki!" Jessie called, pointing that way. She fired twice with her slate-gray, double-action Colt but was too late to keep one of the dark knights from skewering a Ute on his lance.

The warrior threw back his head and screamed to the starlit skies as the knight charged on, trampling over the body of the Ute. Jessie rose, thumbing loads rapidly into her Colt, but by the time the cylinder chambers were filled again, the knight was gone.

Ki had sent an arrow flying after one of the knights, but it had been an act of futility, and he was silently cursing himself for it. Even Ki could give in to anger, to hatred.

The cartel had come to kill. The guns had no particular target. Anything that lived upon the land would do. Just so someone was killed.

The night was silent again.

"Ki?" Jessie whispered.

"Sh!"

"Will they be back?"

She didn't have the chance to get a response before the dark knights came charging out of the woods and the gunfire erupted again.

# Chapter 15

The knights charged through the Indians who still hadn't managed to get out of the clearing, pinned down as they had been by hostile gunfire. Ki saw another Ute impaled on a dark lance.

Teutonic Knights. He knew that one's armor, knew the purple and black silks he wore. Jessie fired twice but apparently missed. Ki waited. The arrows, as the Indians had discovered, would do no good against the ancient armor.

The guns from the woods to Ki's left had stopped briefly for some reason, but now they opened up again with a vengeance and the Utes who had been caught in the open had no choice but to hit the ground again, press their bodies to the dark earth, hoping that they wouldn't be tagged by the flying .44s. There wasn't much chance of that lasting forever with the moon bright and the ground clear. One by one they would be hit—unless they took a long chance and darted for safety.

Ki saw what was happening.

"I'm going to try to draw their fire."

"Ki!"

"Jessica, they have them trapped."

She didn't argue. Ki put his bow and arrow down and moved off as lightly as a cat through the oaks. The gunfire roared on and Jessie did her best to answer it, but it wasn't much of a contest. When her pistol opened up, the rifles trained themselves on her, blasting away, tearing the heavy bark from the oak tree, until Jessie had to cover up and hit the ground herself.

Ki kept moving.

He wanted a diversion to help get the Utes out of the open. The best diversion, he had discovered, was to attack. Nothing takes a man's mind off killing like being threatened with death.

Ki was a dark, floating shadow through the trees. The first cartel thug he came up against never knew what happened. He lifted his eyes from the sights of his Winchester and Ki kicked him in the face. The man sagged back with a faint sigh.

He saw the man's bay then, a big sleek animal—well, the criminals seemed to be able to afford the best horses. But then they needed them.

Ki looked twice at the man on the ground. Dead. His neck had been broken and it satisfied Ki—he wouldn't do what he had in mind to a living man, not even to a cartel hireling.

He lifted the dead man on to his horse, propped him up with a stick shoved down his shirt, and tied it to the pommel with a rawhide string. His feet were quickly strapped to the stirrups. Then Ki scooped up dead leaves from the ground and shoved them up the man's sleeves, down his pants, in his pockets, while beyond the trees the firing continued furiously.

"Good-bye, my friend," Ki said as he struck a match. "This will prepare you for your eternity." He touched the match to the dry leaves and the man blazed into fiery life.

Ki slapped the bay's haunch and the human torch rode out into the clearing, all afire.

A shout went up from the trees and then a series of startled cries, loud curses, and one peculiarly feminine scream. Someone panicked and fired a shot at the human torch who now rode among the cartel men.

It was all the Utes needed to scramble to safety. They broke for the rocks and trees, and although Ki saw two warriors go down and one limping badly, most of them made it.

Behind the concealed badmen, Ki continued to work his way in the opposite direction. He found his next victim reloading his rifle. A tall man with a narrow face whose lip curled up as he saw Ki, he slapped at his holster, trying for his sidearm. It never cleared leather. A *shuriken* spinning from Ki's hand caught the thug in the throat, and he went down—sprawled, bloody, and dead.

Ki picked up the rifle and went on.

The firing had grown even more intense. Tongues of flames streaked the night. Ki came across a cartel man with an arrow in his chest. The man was dying, but he had strength to say, "Give me a . . . give me . . ." and then he was dead.

Ki shook his head and went on. Quickly he hit the ground—suddenly, silently. Two cartel men were hurrying toward him, running in a crouch. They hadn't seen Ki yet, and when they did, it was too late.

Ki's hand snaked out and grabbed the first man's ankle,

yanking him to the ground. Before the other could turn and analyze the situation, Ki, using a rifle like a club, slammed the man's skull. He dropped like a poleaxed steer and Ki finished the man on the ground. That one lifted his head, took a side kick in the face, and sagged back.

Ki disarmed them and threw their weapons away, after first selecting a second rifle to give the Utes.

The shooting had slowed as both sides settled into a sniping battle. Ki started back in the opposite direction, figuring he had pressed his luck far enough. He found Jessica at the big oak, her pistol in her hands.

"Well, you took your time," she said, but there was relief in her voice.

"I met some friends."

"And you stopped to toast them?" Jessie asked.

"Just one. Where's Chi-Tha?"

"I'm not sure. There's a dozen of his people through the trees there."

Ki looked that way and, showing Jessie the rifles, trotted to the Indian position. "You might want these," Ki told them.

"If the man in armor comes back," one young brave told him, "I will want this. You showed us he is human when your arrow found its mark. Now let us see if he can be killed by a bullet."

Ki grinned, patted the man's shoulder, and scurried back to Jessica's position. She glanced up at him. Before them and to their left a spate of gunfire drew their eyes.

"This is going to take a long time, Ki."

"Like this, yes." He looked at the moon and back at Jessica. "The cartel people aren't going to pull out. They're here to do a job and they'll fight until they've been beaten or they've killed every Ute."

"Nobody's going to break this one up."

"Then there is only one thing to do—win," Ki said. "Attack and beat them off."

"Attack? With this force?"

"Why not? We have the silent people, the silent feet, the silent weapons."

"They've got the guns and the numbers."

"Neither will help them in the dark." Ki again looked at the moon. "When that goes down, just before dawn—that will be the time to attack."

"Yes," she said, her voice distant.

"What are you thinking of?" A scattering of shots lifted Ki's eyes. He saw no target for his arrows, so he returned his attention to Jessica. "Him?"

"Him?" She gave a little laugh. "Yes, Reggie. We'll know tomorrow, won't we? Know which one it was."

"Yes. Tomorrow."

"You can't very well hide a missing eye, can you, Ki?" she said.

"No. But do you think it was Reggie?" he asked with surprise.

"I don't know. I'm afraid it was. He has a cave in the hills with a horse and armor hidden in it."

"Yes."

"That other armor—I'm afraid it looked a lot like what the knight was wearing tonight."

"It means nothing in itself."

"No. Nothing." She didn't care to discuss it any longer. At the sound of rifles from the cartel position, she began to empty her revolver methodically at the muzzle flashes. She had at least one hit. A savage howl of pain drifted to their ears. Jessie nodded with satisfaction and they settled in for a long wait.

The moon rolled slowly past and then went dark as the Rocky Mountains sheltered it. Ki had called the Utes together and they seemed to know what he wanted them to do, seemed to feel that they could do it.

"This isn't the time for guns," Ki said in a quiet voice. "It's time to return to the old ways. We will fight silently. Kill silently."

There wasn't any more to say. There were no questions from the Utes.

"Now?" Jessie asked.

"There is no better time," Ki replied. "Jessie..."

"I'm going," she said.

"This isn't your type of battle. Hand to hand with men."

Jessie smiled. "It's my type of battle. It's against the cartel."

Ki gave up the argument. He had tried to win many such discussions in the past. None had worked very well. "Then, take this," he said, handing Jessica his bow and arrows.

Chi-Tha asked, *"She* can use these? A white woman?"

"This white woman can," Ki assured the Ute leader. "I taught her myself." He looked to the other Indians gathered around him. "It is time, I think. Let's go—silently."

The Indians began to circle out from the trees, taking up their positions. The night had gone dark and by the feeble starlight it wasn't possible to see anyone more than a few feet away. That was what Ki had wanted—stealth and darkness were their allies.

"Which way for me?" Jessie asked.

"With me."

"When?"

"As soon as the flanks are covered. Five minutes, no more."

It was closer to three when Ki rose from the crouch he had assumed to nod at Jessie. He had the cool *shuriken* in his hand, their flat, razor-edged steel comforting, familiar.

Moving through the trees in the darkness, Ki didn't have

much chance to watch Jessie, but he glanced back from time to time, amazed as always at the woman's pure nerve and her dedication to removing the cartel vermin from this country.

Ki and Jessie were behind the cartel position now and a stroke of luck came their way. A horse nickered and, veering that way, they found a string of horses. The cartel had left them without a guard as they crept up on the Ute camp.

"Cut them free at that end," Ki said, and Jessie moved off. There were twenty or twenty-five horses in the string. Maybe there were more hidden somewhere, but now at least that many cartel men wouldn't be able to run if the going got tough.

Ki meant to see that it got tough.

With a *shuriken*, he cut loose the other end of the long string, and then he and Jessie silently shooed the horses away. It was far enough. They would run when the lead started to fly.

"Which way?" Jessie asked. Her hair was streaked by starlight, her eyes bright with it.

"The gully," Ki told her. "It should bring us up behind the gunmen."

"I don't see any of the Utes; I don't hear them."

"Then," Ki said, "everything is well."

He started up the gully, moving swiftly through the brush. His feet made barely a whisper against the earth. He could hear the brush scratching against Jessie's clothing, but she, too, was silent, silent enough to escape detection by most.

About now the cartel gunhands were tired. Dawn was nearly here and they had been at it for hours. Also, they could not be expecting an attack form the Utes. Knowing the Indians were underarmed, they probably had been surprised at meeting any resistance whatever. The Indians, after all, had families to consider. They had been expected to

161

break and run, stampeded into flight by the firepower of the intruders.

It hadn't worked that way. The cartel had expected a quick victory, but they weren't going to get it. If Ki and Jessica could do anything about it, they would gain no victory at all.

Ki flattened himself against the ground. He had nearly run into a cartel camp. Seven or eight men slept, while two more sat guard. They were planning on attacking at dawn, then, and were now trying to get some rest.

"Good," Ki said to himself. It fit him perfectly. Men waking from a heavy sleep weren't fighting men—they were only targets.

Jessie wriggled up beside Ki. He was aware of her scent, of powder and soap, despite the long day and longer night, aware of the warmth of her body. She rolled to him and whispered in his ear. "When?"

Ki shook his head. "When it begins," was all he told her. The Utes should be in their positions by now. Ki would leave the moment to Chi-Tha. When the first arrow flew, then it would begin; when the first man died, then they would fight until no one was left alive—on either side.

The minutes dragged. Ki grew chilled and stiff. He had trained himself to be patient—patience is second only to training in a warrior's skills—but it wasn't easy on this night. He wanted to have at it, to throw himself at the cartel's throat, to tear the jugular from it. This mad game had gone on too long.

Knights and castles and tournaments and Spanish curses and burning men—all spun through his mind briefly until Ki, reaching deep within for the self-control he had been given long ago by the masters who had taught him, pulled himself together with slow, cadenced breathing, with soft

162

chanting, controlling the body with the mind—as it was meant to do.

The first arrow flew unexpectedly. Yet Ki saw it. He saw the spinning white feathers, saw the arrow strike one of the two guards above him. A war whoop sounded from the woods. It was against Ki's orders to yell, but the blood of the Ute had been stirred, and the ancient war whoop flowed joyously. Now the battle had begun.

Now many would die.

★

# Chapter 16

The first guard doubled up and spilled forward on to his face, his unfired rifle still on his lap. The second rose and was shot by another Ute. His rifle discharged into the air, and that combined with the war whoop brought the sleeping men out of their blankets in a hurry.

Ki glanced at Jessie, saw that she had notched and aimed an arrow, and started forward, *shuriken* in hand as the darting shadows of the Indians moved silently through the oak woods.

Jessie's arrow sang past him and struck a thick-chested cartel gunman in the gut. He sat looking at it incredulously for a long minute before he flopped back, twitching in the dirt.

Ki vaulted the body, flung a death-dealing *shuriken* into the face of a rising cartel thug, and then with a flying *tobi-geri* kick took the fight out of a second thug, his lead foot

165

striking throat muscles and sending the cartel henchman sprawling.

Wisely, Jessica had held her position and was firing from ambush. Even as Ki looked her way he saw an arrow fly from her bow, one which tagged a cartel man in his gun arm. He slapped at his arm and roared a curse. From the trees a Ute arrow finished him.

Ki fought on. He found three more dead men, all cartel people. He was aware of many bodies moving through the night around him; he could hear their whispered passage, feel the heat of their bodies, nearly sense their determination as the Utes struck back in defense of their home.

He heard a distant rumbling which eluded his logic briefly until he recalled the string of horses. Panicked by gunfire, untethered, they were on the run now, leaving the cartel men to face the Utes or flee afoot.

A silhouette showed itself against the sky and Ki, recognizing that it was no Ute, flung a *shuriken* toward the man. He toppled like a target in a shooting gallery. Ki ran on, not stopping to retrieve his throwing star for he had seen something else which intrigued him much more, which lifted his blood to a raging boil.

The knight was there.

How he was fighting with his damaged eye, Ki couldn't guess, but there he was, a dark figure on a dark horse. He was cutting his way through a group of four Utes who were apparently still armed only with bows and arrows. His broadsword cut left and right and two Utes went down, one wounded seriously.

Ki burst into the small clearing and the knight turned his horse instantly, charging down on Ki.

He had a sword in his hand and Ki looked like meat waiting to be butchered. Ki wasn't going to let it happen. The thundering dark charger was nearly on top of Ki before

166

he leaped aside and snatched at the knight's sword arm.

The silvery blade sliced air above Ki's head, but ducking and moving with the agility of a cat, Ki snatched a wrist and yanked.

The knight started to topple as the horse raced on. Before the knight reached the trees, he hit the ground and Ki was darting toward him. It had to be his hands, *te;* the *shuriken* were useless against an armored man. The knight was on his feet already and from his belt he drew another formidable weapon.

The head of the mace whooshed through the air as the knight gave Ki fair warning of his intent. The spiked head of the weapon, designed to cave in a helmet, could crush Ki's skull—it could also smash ribs, shatter arm bones.

The knight was stalking him now, moving in, circling. Ki was trying to measure his man. He knew he had speed on the knight and maneuverability, but that mace wasn't a toy to be played with, not if the man knew what to do with it, and all of the men who could be the black knight were experts with medieval weapons.

"You can't win," Ki said. "Why not give it up now? Your men are beaten."

The knight wouldn't answer. Still, he wouldn't risk giving his identity away.

He stepped in and the mace hummed past Ki's head as Ki dived to one side and rolled away. Coming up, he had to duck again immediately, hitting the earth. Ki backed off and came up once more, assuming his position, legs crouched, hands loose on extended arms. The knight came in, the mace head tracing figure eights through the air, the spiked ball like a darting steel moon in the semidarkness.

Ki was still watching, waiting, timing the flight of the mace.

The knight was in close enough to try it now and he

167

yelled as he tried to club Ki with the mace. But Ki's hands were quicker. He stepped forward only inches and caught the mace's chain just behind the head. He yanked and kicked out at once, his foot meeting the knight's vulnerable groin.

The mace came free in his hands and Ki winged it aside. The knight was just straightening up, breathing raggedly. He gargled a curse and came in again, a black dagger in his hand.

Ki wove to one side as the knife flashed downward; he took the knight at the wrist and twisted. The dark knight went down in a heap, wrist bone cracking, armor jangling.

"Now," Ki panted. "Remove your helmet."

"Go to hell," the knight spat, and then he resorted to something not exactly medieval. He pulled a small revolver from somewhere and a bullet whipped past Ki's head. Ki still had the knight's dagger in his hand. Now, dropping to the ground, he drove up and under the knight's helmet, finding jugular.

The knight died under him and Ki, on his knees, wiped back his hair, breathed slowly, and watched the stars.

Jessica was there suddenly and Ki smiled at her. "Who . . . ?" she asked but Ki couldn't tell her yet.

"The fight, how does it go?" he asked.

"The Utes have won, or are winning. They took a dozen sleeping men down by the river."

Ki nodded. Was he deliberately putting off the moment? He told her, "Let's see then who we have."

He unstrapped the helmet and tugged and the head fell free, bloodied, shapeless in death.

"Von Rundstedt," Jessica said and the name came out with a relieved exhalation.

"Yes."

"It had to be him, didn't it? Who else could it have been?" Jessie asked.

"I don't know who else it is," Ki said as he rose dusting his hands off, wiping them on his jeans.

"Is? I don't understand, Ki."

"Don't you? Look again."

She did. It was quite simple—Von Rundstedt had both of his eyes. The other knight, the one Ki wounded, had to have one bad eye.

"One of the others."

"So it seems."

Jessie said very softly, "Damn," and then there wasn't much to say.

The battle was nearly over. They heard distant shots as the Utes pursued some of the fleeing cartel men into the hills, but nearby things were secure enough that there was a campfire in the village and the women and children were already returning as Jessie and Ki arrived.

Chi-Tha greeted them like family this time. He was flushed with victory. "It is done! We have won a great battle."

"It is done. Your men are fighters, Chi-Tha," Ki told the Ute.

"Yes, yes, but it took you to jab at us, to prod us."

"No one but a fool is eager to fight," Ki responded. "Have you many casualties?"

"Six dead," Chi-Tha said soberly. "Twice that number injured, but it was the price we had to pay, was it not?"

"I'm afraid so," Ki answered.

"The Spanish ghost—you killed him?" the Ute leader asked.

"I killed a man in armor," Ki said.

"Then it is over. It is ended. Stay with us now, both of you, and feast with us. Let us dance and eat and then sleep the sleep of the victors."

"Thank you for your offer," Jessica said, "but it isn't quite over for us."

169

"No?" Chi-Tha's eyes narrowed with interest.

"There is another man," Ki explained, "one who was the leader of this scheme. We haven't yet found him."

"But this man—you will know him when you find him?" the Indian asked.

"We will know him."

"And then," Chi-Tha said hopefully, "you will kill him so that this cannot happen again."

"And then," Ki agreed, "we will kill him."

They had already begun their feast, the drums thumping, bone whistles shrilling, warriors dancing, when Jessica and Ki rode wearily out of the Ute camp in the White River Basin and followed the trail toward the hills and the castle beyond.

"You still think it's Reggie, don't you?" Jessie asked from out of the darkness.

"I've given up conjecture. We'll know soon enough," Ki replied.

Jessica couldn't get it out of her mind, however; she speculated, "Ethelbert—it could easily be him. Remember all that talk at the dinner party about rounding up the peasants and putting them into labor camps? He was sure Von Rundstedt would support him."

"He was drunk," Ki said.

"Odd idea anyway, and a dangerous one. He needs the money, doesn't he?"

Ki didn't want to be drawn into the discussion. He had spoken the truth—he had given up conjecture. They would find a one-eyed knight and that would be that.

"Sato—didn't he threaten to kill you? Isn't he a warrior for hire?"

"Jessica, please."

"All right." She fell silent again, guiding her horse up the narrow trail through shoulder-high sage and sumac. Ki was right. There was nothing to be gained by worrying. Maybe she was just trying to find a way to place the blame on Reggie, who was after all still the most logical one, Reggie who was out at night on mysterious errands, who had horse and armor hidden away, who painted pictures of himself as the dark knight. Reggie who . . . Jessie forced all the spinning thoughts from her mind. She looked at the dark trail and did everything possible to keep from thinking at all.

It was dawn when they reached the castle.

There was dew on the grass, sparkling brilliantly in rainbow hues. The mountains were withdrawing now from the purple haze of night to become bright, stolid giants.

The fair had left a profusion of litter across the grounds, bottles, broken kegs, candy apple wrappers. The tents, their colors not yet brightened by the sun, seemed damp and forlorn.

The lists drew Jessica's attention briefly—the lists where on this morning someone was scheduled to die.

Would Sir John insist on going through with that now that Von Rundstedt was dead? He had only Sato, Ethelbert and Reggie . . . no, he had only two men.

For one of them had lost an eye during the night. And that one would die without going through the rituals of battle.

# Chapter 17

It was dark in the castle, dark and musty and still.

There was no sound of daily activity. There didn't seem to be a servant in the place, a laborer, a guest. Nothing, but perhaps the ghosts of the castle, stirred.

"What do you want to do, Ki?" Jessie asked, her voice lowering to a whisper.

"Find the man. Find him now and be done with this," Ki replied.

"All right. We split up?"

"Yes. So long as you have your pistol."

Jessie laughed but the laughter didn't reach her eyes. "I'm not going to be without it so long as we're here, Ki. Don't worry about that."

"If you do find him—whoever he is—wait for me to help you, please."

"Sure," she said and Ki almost believed her.

There was someone stirring upstairs now. They could

hear shuffling feet, the sound of splashing water. Jessica glanced at Ki.

"I think that's Reggie's room."

"Or Ethelbert's."

"Ki . . . I want to find out by myself. If it's Reggie, I don't think he'll try to hurt me. Don't ask me why, I just don't think so."

"Talk to the man then," Ki said. Jessie frowned, unable to believe that Ki had given in so easily.

He had his reasons, however. Jessie hadn't seen it, but Ki had. Spots of blood across the stone floor of the great hall leading toward the dungeon door. Whoever was upstairs splashing wasn't the injured knight. That one had made his way downward.

"Ki?" Jessie peered at him questioningly.

"Go talk to the man if you must. Do it your way, Jessie."

Still looking quizzically at Ki, she started off, moving slowly at first, then striding lightly, rapidly, up the staircase to the upper floor. What did Ki have on his mind? It was odd for him not to argue if he believed she were putting herself in danger. Maybe he now had reason to believe that it wasn't Reggie.

"Don't let it be him," she said to the empty stone corridor. Still, her hand gripped her pistol tightly as she neared his room.

The door was open just a hair and Jessica eased up to it, peering in. Reggie was there, his shirt off, standing at his basin. He was holding a towel to his face.

Jessie briefly sagged back against the wall, frustrated, even angry. Angry with herself and Reggie Whitechapel. She was a Starbuck, however, and she pulled herself together, toed open the door, and stepped inside, her .38 Colt's barrel coming level.

"Stand still, Reggie," she said quietly, and the man froze.

Jessie took several steps forward. "Good," she told him. "Now take that towel away from your face and turn around."

He did, but so slowly that Jessie ached. The towel came down to reveal a freshly shaven, handsome face with both eyes intact. Jessica Starbuck felt her knees go soft on her and the gun came down.

"Oh, damn you, Reggie Whitechapel," she whispered.

"Jessica, what is it?"

He crossed the room, throwing the towel aside. Then he was holding her in his strong, warrior's arms, his bare chest pressed against her. He smelled of shaving soap. "Just what is wrong here, woman?" he asked, brushing back a strand of her blond hair.

"I thought it was you," she said. She was still angry— and she stepped back, wriggling from his arms. She crossed to his bed and sat on it, holding her pistol between her knees. "I thought it was you, that's all. You didn't have to make yourself so suspicious, did you?"

"Do I know what you're talking about?" Reggie asked lightly.

"I don't know," she sighed. "You have to have some idea what I'm talking about. You're not deaf and dumb, you're not stupid. I'm talking about what's going on around this castle, Reggie. Your hidden horse, your hidden armor, your midnight rides—"

"Jessie—" He came forward but her pistol came up again.

"No." She shook her head strongly. "Don't touch me, Reggie. I want you to, but don't touch me until you've told me what you know about all of this, about why you've been acting this way."

"All right," he answered, "you win."

And he told her all about it.

175

Ki moved cautiously to the panel in the wall, and he had to search for a few minutes before he found the spot he sought, and pressing it, he saw the panel slide back.

There was darkness beyond the panel, but somewhere a light glowed dimly, briefly, and then it was extinguished. Ki smiled. He had his man.

He started forward. There was a torch on the wall in an iron bracket and he briefly debated with himself—darkness or light, which was the better ally.

In the end he struck a match and lit the torch. He didn't know the dungeon and its railless spiral staircase, and although he was also illuminating himself, he had to take the chance.

There were spots of blood on the stone, nearly dry now, and once a smeared bloody handprint on the wall. Ki moved forward stealthily, eyes searching the darkness, which was overpowering despite the flickering efforts of the torch that sent up more smoke than flame and smelled strongly of coal oil.

Something moved and Ki froze, drawing a *shuriken* from one of his vest pockets. It was only a rat, huge and black, scuttling away.

The torch cast wavering shadows against the stone walls; the air grew cool. There was an unhealthy smell in the damp air.

Ki reached the dungeon floor and he waited, just listening and watching. If there were any spirits in the castle, they were here, here where ancient instruments of torture rested, where rusted chains set into the stone walls bore mute testimony to past horrors, to past blood.

He came out of the darkness with his sword raised, slashing at the air beside Ki's head. Ki threw himself backward, flinging the torch at the attacking knight's face, at the face with only a single eye.

At the face of Sir John Whitechapel.

"Bastard," he croaked at Ki who had risen into a crouch and now waited defensively for the madman to attack again. The sputtering, fallen torch illuminated Whitechapel's distorted face. The tendons on his throat stood taut; his mouth was twisted.

"Why?" Ki asked.

*"Why?"* The voice that repeated the question wasn't really human. Dry, distant, cracked by pain and madness, it reflected the character of the man who spoke, for Sir John Whitechapel was mad, had always been mad. A feeling that Ki had carried with him from the start, that there was madness behind this, had proven in the end to be right.

"Yes, why did you do this? Why fall in with the cartel? You've known about them for years, of course, a merchant of your experience."

"I always knew about them. They approached me. They knew I needed money."

"How could you?"

"Do you know what this castle costs? Guess what it requires to move it stone by stone to Colorado from England and reassemble it! Besides I never had the money my son thought I did, that my stepbrother Ethelbert hoped I did."

"Then why throw it away?" Ki asked.

Whitechapel was hunched forward, sword drooping in his hand, his eye trickling blood across his aristocratic face.

"Throw it away!" Whitechapel stiffened. "On establishing the order of things—the order of things as they used to be, need to be!"

"Feudalism."

177

"Feudalism if you want to call it that, society where class rules, where the peasants keep their place, where . . . you wouldn't understand."

"Wouldn't I? I think I do. I've seen this system in Japan, seen remnants of it in America. It never worked; it never will."

Whitechapel didn't seem to have heard him. "I was sorry, of course, that the Starbuck girl had to be involved, that she will have to be killed in the end—Alex Starbuck was a man. To kill his daughter will not be easy, but Von Rundstedt could have taken care of that—he's been very efficient in the past they tell me."

"At murder."

"You don't understand, do you?"

Ki said quietly, "I think I do. I think I understand madness when I see it."

Whitechapel blanched. "Madness?" he repeated. *"Madness?"* and then he cut out at Ki with the broadsword again and Ki had to do it. He sent a deadly *shuriken* singing toward the crazed knight, and Whitechapel staggered back, falling against the floor where he lay drifting into his dark dreams before he died.

Ki turned and walked away. What else was there to do?

He found Jessie and Reggie at the head of the stairs.

"Ki . . ." Reggie asked.

"Yes. I had to do it."

Reggie sagged a little, shaking his head. "I knew it. I should have stopped it. I tried to—tried to cover for him— tried to reason with him. When his horse would come in sweaty, I would rub it down. I would clean the blood from his lances. I would ride out myself at midnight to stop him. I kept armor and a horse hidden in the hills to combat him after he took to having my good armor, my best horse put away." The dark-eyed man went on, "I jousted with him

178

more than once on the dark prairie and sent him home, turned him back."

"You knew it all," Ki said.

"Guessed it all—as I told Jessie. After a while, I knew."

"But you didn't stop him."

"I did the best I could. What was I to do? Commit him? Have you ever seen an asylum? I have—three of my blood relatives have gone mad. What was I to do? Kill him? He was my father! No matter what else he was, he was my father, Ki, and I could never do such a thing. I tried to protect the people, tried to protect him as well. It was an effort doomed to failure."

"And now?" Ki asked.

"And now," Reggie said, lifting his eyes, "I'll have this doomed and dismal monument torn down. I swear it—torn down."

His fists were clenched and neither Jessie nor Ki could say anything to the tormented young man. The young man who feared madness was in his blood.

There was little left to do but depart, to leave the White-chapels to their fates. Jessie was silent and withdrawn as they prepared to leave. Ki couldn't offer any consolation worth having.

"What, I wonder," Jessica asked, "is a knight's funeral like?"

Ki had finished saddling his horse. He now checked the bridle straps once more, tightening the throat latch one notch. A shadow from across the stable raised his eyes.

Sato stood there, empty-handed. He was watching Ki, just watching.

"Well, Sato—" Ki's voice was weary. "You have said we would fight to the death. Is it to be now?"

"No." Sato came forward a little. "I have seen your work. I do not fear dying, but I don't want to take the life of a

179

warrior such as you. We are, after all, warrior brothers, are we not?"

"No," Ki said coldly, "we are not. You will never understand fighting for anything but profit. I will never understand a man who draws blood for the sake of gold. We are not warrior brothers. Don't use that as an excuse for not fighting me.

"How will it be, Sato? Will we fight?"

"No," Sato said, but his eyes were savage. "We will not fight." Under his breath he added, "Not this time, not now."

Then there was nothing left to say or do at Whitechapel Castle or in the White River Basin, so Jessica Starbuck and Ki rode slowly out through the gate of the dying, gray castle. Only once did she look back hoping to catch a last glimpse of the young, dark-eyed man who walked the empty parapets of the castle, master of all he surveyed.

Explore the exciting Old West with
one of the men who made it wild!

| | | |
|---|---|---|
| ___07543-4 | LONGARM IN DEADWOOD #45 | $2.50 |
| ___07425-X | LONGARM AND THE GREAT TRAIN ROBBERY #46 | $2.50 |
| ___07418-7 | LONGARM IN THE BADLANDS #47 | $2.50 |
| ___07414-4 | LONGARM IN THE BIG THICKET #48 | $2.50 |
| ___07522-1 | LONGARM AND THE EASTERN DUDES #49 | $2.50 |
| ___07854-9 | LONGARM IN THE BIG BEND #50 | $2.50 |
| ___07523-X | LONGARM AND THE SNAKE DANCERS #51 | $2.50 |
| ___07722-4 | LONGARM ON THE GREAT DIVIDE #52 | $2.50 |
| ___08101-9 | LONGARM AND THE BUCKSKIN ROGUE #53 | $2.50 |
| ___07723-2 | LONGARM AND THE CALICO KID #54 | $2.50 |
| ___07545-0 | LONGARM AND THE FRENCH ACTRESS #55 | $2.50 |
| ___08099-3 | LONGARM AND THE OUTLAW LAWMAN #56 | $2.50 |
| ___07859-X | LONGARM AND THE BOUNTY HUNTERS #57 | $2.50 |
| ___07858-1 | LONGARM IN NO MAN'S LAND #58 | $2.50 |
| ___07886-7 | LONGARM AND THE BIG OUTFIT #59 | $2.50 |
| ___08259-7 | LONGARM AND SANTA ANNA'S GOLD #60 | $2.50 |
| ___08388-7 | LONGARM AND THE CUSTER COUNTY WAR #61 | $2.50 |
| ___08161-2 | LONGARM IN VIRGINIA CITY #62 | $2.50 |
| ___08369-0 | LONGARM AND THE JAMES COUNTY WAR #63 | $2.50 |

Prices may be slightly higher in Canada.

5